Elsie's
New
Life

Elsie's New Life

BOOK THREE

of the
A Life of Faith:
Elsie Dinsmore
Series

Based on the beloved books by
Martha Finley

Mission City Press
Franklin, Tennessee

Book Three of the *A Life of Faith: Elsie Dinsmore* Series

Elsie's New Life
Copyright © 1999, Mission City Press, Inc.
All Rights Reserved.

Published by Mission City Press, Inc.

This series is based on the bestselling *Elsie Dinsmore* novels written by Martha Finley and first published in 1868 by Dodd, Mead & Company.

Cover & Interior Design: Richmond & Williams, Nashville, Tennessee
Cover Photography: Michelle Grisco Photography, West Covina, California
Typesetting: BookSetters, White House, Tennessee

Special Thanks to Glen Eyrie Castle and Conference Center, Colorado Springs, Colorado, for Photo Shoot Locations.

Unless otherwise indicated, all Scripture references are from the Holy Bible New International Version (NIV). Copyright © 1973, 1978, 1984 by International Bible Society. Used by permission of Zondervan Publishing House, Grand Rapids, MI. All rights reserved.

Elsie Dinsmore and *A Life of Faith* are trademarks of Mission City Press, Inc.

For more information, write to Mission City Press at P.O. Box 681913, Franklin, Tennessee 37068-1913, or visit our Web Site at

www.alifeoffaith.com

Library of Congress Catalog Card Number: 99-65156
Finley, Martha
    Elsie's New Life
    Book Three of the *A Life of Faith: Elsie Dinsmore* Series
    ISBN 1-928749-03-8

Printed in the United States of America
3 4 5 6 7 8 — 05 04 03 02 01

DEDICATION

This book is
dedicated to
the memory of
MARTHA FINLEY

*May the rich legacy of
pure and simple devotion to Christ
that she introduced through
Elsie Dinsmore in 1868
live on in our day and
in generations to come.*

— FOREWORD —

*N*o one could have been more surprised by the success of *Elsie Dinsmore* than her creator, Martha Finley. A teacher who had turned to full-time writing just before the Civil War, Miss Finley believed her book would be a one-time effort. She fully expected to turn her attention to other subjects after *Elsie*'s publication. But her public had different ideas.

Published in two volumes in 1868 and 1869, *Elsie Dinsmore* became what we now call an 'overnight sensation', and readers all across the United States were soon clamoring for more stories about Elsie, the little girl of big faith. The book's publisher happily agreed, so Miss Finley, who had spent three years writing her first *Elsie Dinsmore* novel, quickly went back to her pen and paper. Her next story followed Elsie into girlhood and adolescence — "the years," Miss Finley said, "in which her character was developing, and mind and body were growing and strengthening for the real work and battle of life."

Now, more than a century after Elsie's first appearance, Mission City Press is pleased to continue Miss Finley's saga in *Elsie's New Life*, the third in the *Elsie Dinsmore: A Life of Faith* series. This version has been faithfully adapted and carefully updated from Miss Finley's original, so that modern readers will find Elsie's story as fresh, exciting, and relevant to Christians today as it was in the late 19th century.

Elsie's New Life

In Book Two of the series, *Elsie's Impossible Choice*, Elsie's emotional struggle to win her father's love came to its dramatic conclusion. Faced with tragedy and unbearable loss, Horace Dinsmore, Jr., at last invited the Lord into his heart and was united with his daughter by the power of God's love and forgiveness. As *Elsie's New Life* opens, Horace and Elsie are beginning their new life together, and readers will follow Elsie from age ten to sixteen. With her unwavering Christian faith and the love of her father to guide her, Elsie will confront changes in her family, meet new people and experience new places, and accept the challenges of adolescence. But the road is not always straight and smooth, and Elsie will discover that growing up brings new dilemmas and difficult decisions.

Martha Finley always hoped that Elsie's adventures would serve as an example and inspiration for all Christian young people and their parents. As her stories now reach out to readers in a new millenium, Miss Finley's hope is indeed being rewarded, and Mission City Press is proud to be part of the on-going success of Elsie Dinsmore.

✎ SLAVERY IN ELSIE'S WORLD ✎

The fictional Elsie Dinsmore was born in the South in the 1830s, and she grew up amid families whose wealth and social standing depended on their ownership of slaves. It is difficult for readers today to understand what slavery was like or how it could have been allowed in a nation founded on the principle that "all men are created equal." But the truth is that slavery existed almost from the beginning of America's history and was ended only by the Civil War, also known as the War Between the States, fought from 1861 to 1865.

Foreword

What is slavery? It is hard to give an exact definition because the practice of slavery is ancient, and it varied widely from place to place and time to time. But in general terms, slavery involves the ownership of one human being (the slave) by another (the master). Slavery is a form of forced labor that was practiced even before recorded history, and it has existed in virtually every part of the world at one time or another. Examples of slavery appear frequently in the Bible: the Old Testament tells how the Israelites, for instance, were enslaved by the Pharoahs of Egypt, and only after God brought a series of terrible plagues upon the Egyptians could Moses lead his people to freedom.

Slaves could be obtained in a number of ways — through warfare, kidnapping, enslavement of criminals, purchase from other slave owners or slave traders, and even the sale of oneself or family members. The period of a slave's servitude could be limited to a number of years or last for life. In America, a slave was considered property for life and all of his or her descendants were regarded as slaves from birth. (At Roselands, young Jim, the stable boy who is almost punished for a crime he didn't commit in *Elsie's Endless Wait*, is a slave because his mother, Aunt Phoebe, is a slave.)

In custom and law, slaves were the property of their masters, like cattle or tools or the land itself; therefore, slaves had few if any human rights. In the South of the 1830s, for example, a black slave could not testify against a white person in the courts of law, so if a slave was beaten, robbed, or falsely accused by a white, the slave could not give evidence at his own trial.

Masters controlled where the slaves could go, how they would live and work, what they ate and wore, even whom they could marry and how their families were organized.

Slaves worked at whatever jobs and for however long the master dictated, but they received no payment for their labor. They could be sold at any time, and slave families could be broken apart at a moment's notice. In the South, where slave owners feared that education would lead to rebellion, it was illegal to teach slaves to read or write.

Slaves were usually outsiders — people of a different race, nationality, or ethnic heritage than their masters. As outsiders, they could be classed as inferiors, suited only for hard labor and domestic service. (In America, skin color as well as differences in culture and language made it easy for European settlers to see themselves as "better" than African slaves.) Wherever slavery existed, it had to be protected by a legal system that was under the control of the slave owners. It also had to be accepted by non-slaveholders who were willing to uphold a slave system.

❧ SLAVERY IN THE AMERICAS ❧

When Europeans invaded the New World — South and Central America, the Caribbean islands, and North America — they often enslaved the native peoples they found here. But the Europeans soon needed more workers to do the back-breaking labor of opening wildernesses, tending huge plantations, and mining natural resources, so slaves were brought across the Atlantic Ocean from eastern Africa. African slaves were first imported by South American colonies like Brazil and to work Spanish, Dutch, and English plantations in the West Indies. The first Africans in North America were a group of twenty indentured servants sold in 1619 in the Virginia colony of Jamestown. (Unlike a true slave, indentured servants could eventually purchase their freedom. Many poor Europeans and a few Africans came to the colonies as indentured workers in the 1600s and into the 1700s.)

Africa had been a source of slaves since ancient times, and Europeans had bought and sold African slaves since the 1500s. But the "slave trade" was greatly intensified when the Americas were colonized. It is estimated that some 12 to 15 million Africans were transported to the New World between 1650 and 1850. This number does not include the many thousands of Africans who died in the wars of captivity or perished from the horrendous conditions aboard the slave ships that traveled from Africa's eastern coast to commercial ports throughout the Americas. Native Africans supplied slaves from their own continent — most often from western Africa — but the business of buying and selling was dominated by the Portuguese, followed by the Spanish, Dutch, and English, and by colonial Americans.

Slavery in the Northern Hemisphere was not limited to the Southern colonies. As the demand for slave labor grew in the 1700s, Northern ship owners, sea captains, and slave traders made large fortunes in the business of transporting and selling slaves. At the time of the American Revolution, slavery was legal in all the original thirteen colonies, but the primary market was the Southern states where the economy was based on agriculture and cheap labor was required for the cultivation of large plantations (farms devoted to the production of one or two profitable cash crops such as tobacco, rice, indigo, hemp, and cotton).

When the Founding Fathers — men like George Washington, Thomas Jefferson, Benjamin Franklin — declared the American colonies independent of British rule and then, after their successful Revolution, drafted the

Elsie's New Life

Constitution of the United States, they did not know what to do about slavery. Washington and Jefferson, for example, didn't believe in slavery on principle, yet both men owned slaves, and they were fearful that ending the practice would severely damage the economy and unity of their new nation. They compromised by including in the Constitution a provision that all trade in slaves, though not slave ownership, must be legally ended in 1808. (Illegal slave trading continued, however, and another quarter-million slaves were imported between 1808 and 1860.)

For a while it seemed that slavery might succumb to a natural death: Northern states began to outlaw slavery soon after the Revolutionary War, and even Southerners were seriously questioning the moral, social, and economic value of continuing the practice. A new, anti-slavery movement called "abolitionism" was rising in Europe and the United States, and by the early 1800s, people of strong religious and moral convictions were demanding the total end of slavery and freedom for all slaves.

But something had happened in 1793 that changed everything. Eli Whitney's invention of the cotton gin gave new life to Southern agriculture. Cotton became "King" in the South, and in the early 1800s, plantation culture including slave labor spread rapidly from the Atlantic coast states (Maryland, Virginia, the Carolinas, and Georgia) into the new territories of the Deep South and West (Alabama, Mississippi, Louisiana, Tennessee, Kentucky, Arkansas, Texas, Missouri).

Slaves were so important to agriculture that the size of a plantation was measured not in acres but in the number of slaves owned by the planter. In fact, relatively few Southerners actually owned slaves, and in some pockets of the South, slavery was virtually non-existent. But the wealthy slaveholders had enormous power; they exercised control over the legislatures and legal systems of the Southern states and were dominant voices in the national government as well. Twelve of America's first sixteen presidents were Southerners, and even a "man of the people" like Andrew Jackson of Tennessee was a slave owner.

By the time that Elsie Dinsmore would have been born in the 1830s, slavery had become a central issue in American politics and national life. The anti-slavery movement was growing in the South as well as the North. Abolitionists decried slavery in town meetings, from church pulpits, and in state and national legislatures. Former slaves including Frederick Douglass and Harriet Tubman became leaders in the freedom movement. The "Underground Railway" — not a train but an arduous series of trails, hiding places, and "safe houses" along which escaped slaves were "conducted" from the South to the northern states and Canada — offered freedom for thousands. Harriet Tubman risked her own life nineteen times and personally conducted more than 600 slaves to safety. But the real goal of the abolitionists was to end all forms of legal slavery.

Defenders of the slave system were equally determined to win the national debate and to see that slavery became legal in the new western territories that were being added to the Union. Wealthy slave owners supported crackpot plans to invade Cuba and Central America and create new slave states. The most eloquent supporters of the status quo, men like John C. Calhoun of South Carolina and Georgia-born William Lowndes Yancey, roused a new separatist spirit in the South. Slavery advocates put forth strong economic arguments and even used the Bible to justify what Southerners liked to call their "peculiar institution."

Elsie's New Life

Over the next three decades, compromise would be tried again and again, and each effort at peaceful settlement invariably failed. In the end, only one option remained. It would take a war and the lives of more than 600,000 soldiers on both sides to decide if the United States were to remain a union of one people or to separate into two nations — one free and the other slave-based.

DINSMORE FAMILY TREE

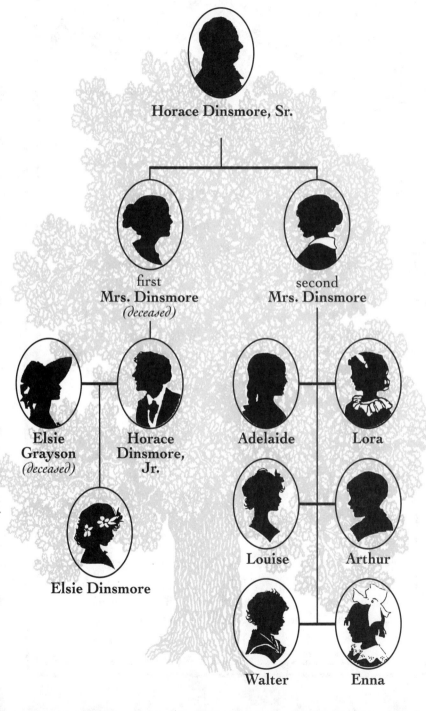

Horace Dinsmore, Sr.

first
Mrs. Dinsmore
(deceased)

second
Mrs. Dinsmore

Elsie
Grayson
(deceased)

Horace
Dinsmore,
Jr.

Adelaide

Lora

Elsie Dinsmore

Louise

Arthur

Walter

Enna

SETTING

$\mathscr{T}$he Oaks, the Old South plantation home of Horace Dinsmore, Jr., and his daughter, Elsie. The story begins in the mid-1840s, about 15 years before the outbreak of the American Civil War.

CHARACTERS

∽ The Oaks ∽

Mr. Horace Dinsmore, Jr. — The only son of Horace Dinsmore, Sr., and his first wife. Once married to the late Elsie Grayson of New Orleans, Horace is a wealthy farmer, businessman, lawyer, and scholar.

Elsie Dinsmore — The only child of Horace Dinsmore, Jr., and Elsie Grayson, who died shortly after Elsie's birth. Elsie has lived in her grandfather's home since she was four years old.

∽ Slaves of The Oaks ∽

Aunt Chloe — The middle-aged nursemaid who has cared for Elsie since birth and taught her in the Christian faith.

Jim — The stable boy who is often responsible for Elsie's safety.

John — Horace Dinsmore, Jr.'s personal servant.

∽ Roselands Plantation ∽

Mr. and Mrs. Horace Dinsmore, Sr. — Elsie's grandfather and his second wife. Their children are **Adelaide, Lora, Louise, Arthur, Walter,** and **Enna.**

∽ Ion Plantation ∽

Edward Travilla — Owner of Ion and friend since boyhood of Horace Dinsmore, Jr.

Mrs. Travilla — Widowed mother of Edward, dedicated Christian, and devoted friend to Elsie.

∽ Ashlands Plantation ∽

Mr. and Mrs. Carrington — Old friends of the Dinsmore family, and parents of twins **Lucy** and **Herbert** and their older brother **Harry**.

Mr. and Mrs. Norris — Mrs. Carrington's elderly parents.

Aunt Viney — The Carringtons' jovial cook.

∽ Philadelphia ∽

Mr. and Mrs. Allison — Friends of the Dinsmore family who live in Philadelphia and also have a summer home, Elmgrove. Mr. Allison is a wealthy merchant. Their children are **Edward**, **Rose** (a close friend of Elsie and Adelaide Dinsmore), **Richard**, **Daniel**, **Sophie**, **Freddie**, **May**, and baby **Daisy**.

Maggie and Hetty — Schoolgirl friends of the young Allisons.

∽ Other Friends & Acquaintances ∽

Mrs. Murray — A Scots Presbyterian woman of deep Christian faith. Elsie's earliest companion, she has been living in her native Scotland for several years.

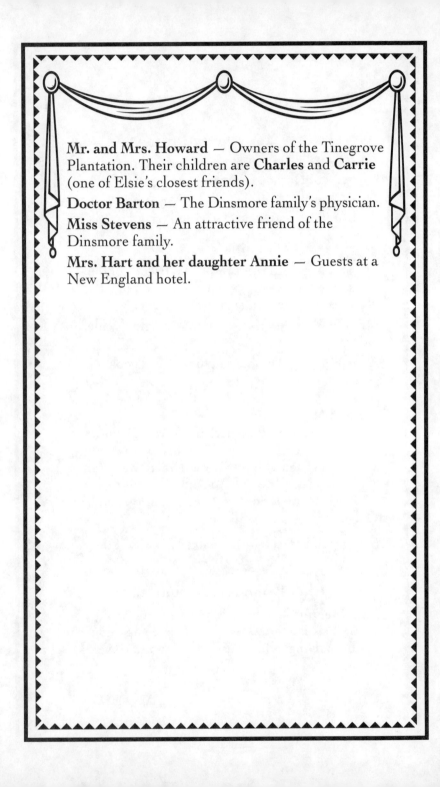

Mr. and Mrs. Howard — Owners of the Tinegrove Plantation. Their children are **Charles** and **Carrie** (one of Elsie's closest friends).

Doctor Barton — The Dinsmore family's physician.

Miss Stevens — An attractive friend of the Dinsmore family.

Mrs. Hart and her daughter Annie — Guests at a New England hotel.

CHAPTER

1

Fresh Starts

"Forget the former things;
do not dwell on the past.
See, I am doing a new thing!
Now it springs up;
do you not perceive it?"

ISAIAH 43:18-19

orace Dinsmore set down his silver-backed hairbrush and looked closely at the reflection of his handsome face in the mirror. Elsie had been right, he thought to himself. Yesterday, she had seen them and asked if they meant he was getting old.

Gray strands, hardly more than two dozen, had appeared in his thick, dark hair. He had never noticed them before. Was he getting old? He had laughed at his daughter's question, gently pinched her cheek, and said, "Oh, yes, Elsie dear, very old. I am all of twenty-eight, and I will soon be feeling the cold and losing my teeth. You will have to wrap me in warm shawls and feed me oatmeal." She had laughed, too — his beautiful, little, hazel-eyed girl whom he had almost lost so soon after finding her.

Now he gazed intently at his new gray hairs and thought, "You are reminders. Each one of you will remind me of my prideful thinking and of all the injustices I inflicted on my poor child, and of my narrow escape from a lifetime of sorrow and regret."

Horace was a man who took great care with his dress and appearance. Even a year ago, the sight of gray in his hair would have shocked him, and he might have been inclined to use a touch of dye to hide them. But now he felt glad of this sprinkling of gray that was like an outward symbol of his inner change and growth.

"And a little child will lead them." Those simple words of Scripture echoed in his mind. Yes, a child had led him. Elsie, only ten years old and so much wiser in the ways of God than he, had led him to a depth of faith and understanding that was literally changing his life. Each day he grew more and more grateful for his salvation — the greatest gift he had ever received.

As he dressed, Horace remembered all that they had come through. Until not quite two years ago, he had never even seen his daughter. At eighteen, Horace had secretly married the most beautiful and kindest young woman, Elsie's mother. But when the marriage was revealed and the young couple were separated by his father and her guardian, Horace had obeyed his father and not his heart. Only after his wife's tragic death did he learn that she had given birth to his child, a daughter named Elsie, after her lovely mother. For eight years he had abandoned his little girl. Oh, he had provided for her security and material well-being, and then assured himself that was the extent of his moral duty to her. But he had gone off to college and later to Europe where he indulged his passions for knowledge and art and travel. He had simply taken his daughter's safety and happiness for granted. It never crossed his mind to be curious about her, even when Elsie had gone to live with his father and stepmother and their large family at Roselands, the plantation where Horace had grown up. It had never occurred to him that his child might be an outcast within his own family.

"What a fool I was!" the young father said aloud to his empty dressing room. "I allowed myself to be misled by my stepmother, but I cannot blame her for my blindness. Even when I finally came home and was united with Elsie, I was too full of pride to trust my child's simple love — too arrogant to respect her deep, abiding faith in God and His love."

It had taken a near-fatal illness to open Horace's eyes and heart. Attempting to impose his authority and break Elsie's

unyielding obedience to the commands of God, Horace had abandoned his little girl a second time. In her grief, Elsie had lost all her strength, and when she contracted a deadly fever, not even Horace's return and his repentance had been enough to save her. For the first time in his life, Horace had turned to his Heavenly Father. And God alone had brought her back.

As images of those painful days — Elsie delirious with fever and screaming in terror at the mere sight of him — again flooded Horace's mind, he knelt where he stood and spoke to the Lord who had so recently become his greatest comfort: "Thank you, God, for sparing me my child. I know that I'm undeserving of Your mercy, for I greatly abused the trust You placed in me. I wandered so far from the path of righteousness, and I shall always be grateful that the Holy Spirit guided me back and led me aright. Dear Lord, help me to be deserving of my child and to train her in Your ways, both by my teachings and my example. And help me to stay on this straight road to Your eternal blessing."

When he had finished his prayer, Horace rose, feeling renewed as he always did now when he took his troubles to God. With a quick glance back to the mirror, he smiled and said, "It's amazing how each new day is to me the grandest source of hope and possibility. Even gray hairs seem a gift to me today." He laughed at himself and hurried to finish dressing, for Elsie would soon be knocking at his door, ready for their morning devotion.

Elsie's recuperation from her illness was slow, and though it had been several months since she passed through the crisis, she had still not recovered her energy. As soon as the doctor had allowed, Horace had moved Elsie from his father's house to their new home at The Oaks, a large and prosperous plantation not far from Roselands. Horace had completely renovated the gracious old estate house, furnishing and decorating each room in exquisite taste and equipping the house with every amenity. A wealthy man in his own right, Horace had spared no expense to make The Oaks perfect for his daughter.

But gilt trimmings and rich fabrics were only the background for the real changes Horace was bringing to his new life with Elsie. Together, father and daughter shared morning and evening devotions — reading the Bible and praying. All her life, Elsie would remember the first time she heard her Papa pray, because knowing that her father had at last opened his heart to Jesus brought her the greatest happiness she had ever felt. Horace also included his new household in his devotions, gathering family and servants together every day for morning and evening worship. And at The Oaks, the Sabbath was observed in accordance with God's command as a day to honor and worship Him.

Horace had, as he once promised, taken over Elsie's schooling, much to her delight, for her father was more widely educated than any governess and knowledgeable in many subjects that other parents thought unnecessary for a young girl to master. When they walked in the garden, he taught her botany. When they rode in the hills, he taught her geology. He instructed her in French and Italian conversation, as well as grammar. In fact, Horace made every subject interesting and rewarded her efforts with praise, so that even memorizing and reciting lessons became a pleasure for Elsie. Horace also encouraged her to resume her music

lessons, for she was a talented young pianist and also blessed with a clear, sweet singing voice. Her domestic instruction was, as always, the duty of her devoted nurse-maid, Aunt Chloe, who helped Elsie with the intricacies of sewing, knitting, and needlework.

Elsie soon got to know all the servants in her new home, though she was most happy to see that Jim, the stable boy who so often served as her attendant when she rode her pony, John, her father's servant, and a few others from Roselands had accompanied them to The Oaks.

Her father also planned an extraordinary surprise on the day he first brought Elsie home to The Oaks — a visit from Mrs. Murray, the elderly Scotswoman who had once served Elsie's mother as housekeeper and nurse. Besides Aunt Chloe, Mrs. Murray was Elsie's oldest friend and companion. A devout Christian, Mrs. Murray had taught Elsie about Jesus, the Bible, and God's eternal love and forgiveness from the time the little girl could begin to understand. She had moved to Roselands with Elsie and protected her young charge as well as she could from the Dinsmore family's coldness and jealousies, but Mrs. Murray had been summoned back to Scotland not long before Horace returned to Roselands, and for two years Elsie had longed to see her dear friend's face once more.

What a wonderful homecoming it was! Horace not only delivered his daughter to a beautiful new house; he reunited her with her beloved Mrs. Murray. How happy Elsie was to hear Mrs. Murray's familiar accent: "Dear, dear bairn," the old lady cried as she rushed down the front steps of The Oaks to enfold Elsie in her gentle embrace. "Ach, but it does my old heart good to see your winsome, wee face once more."

Elsie was overjoyed. "But how did you get here, Mrs. Murray?"

"It was your good father's doing, darling. I arrived last night, just in time to be here to welcome you home," Mrs. Murray replied, holding Elsie at arm's length and examining the little girl's face with her sharp, bright eyes. "But, my, you are looking pale. Well, don't fret, wee girl. We'll soon be getting the roses back into your cheeks."

Taking Mrs. Murray's warm hand, Elsie said softly, "I haven't forgotten any of the good things you taught me."

"I knew you wouldn't," Mrs. Murray said cheerfully. "I knew our precious Lord would always live in your heart."

~~~

Horace found himself impressed by Mrs. Murray, and liking her a great deal. This was something of a revelation because Horace had been led to believe, by his stepmother and his father, that Mrs. Murray was a stern and humorless woman, rigid and self-righteous in her Christian principles. The real person, to the contrary, was both kind and remarkably intelligent, with a quick wit and a love of good conversation.

Far from being self-righteous, she was a true Christian who put her principles into her living, demanded much of herself, and studiously worked to forgive the failings of others. But she was no shrinking violet; there was a streak of steel in Mrs. Murray that made her as courageous as any warrior in the face of injustice and cruelty to others. She was clearly devoted to Elsie, and Horace sensed that Mrs. Murray could be a tigress should any harm threaten his child. As he grew to know her, Horace realized that the seemingly frail

little lady had been Elsie's chief defender and protectress during all those years when he had been absent, and that he owed her a debt of gratitude which could never be fully repaid.

For her part, Mrs. Murray was "a mite suspicious" of Horace at first. She had vivid memories of the hot-headed youth who had so heedlessly pursued, married, and then departed from the first Elsie — leaving that sad young woman to die alone. And he had left Elsie, too, to be raised without the love of a parent. Mrs. Murray and Aunt Chloe had done their best, and both women loved Elsie as if she were their own. But there was no substitute for the love of a parent, and Horace had, of his own choosing, deprived Elsie of that love for so many years.

But the Horace she encountered at The Oaks was a man of maturity, who, she sensed, was doing everything in his power to make amends for his youthful callousness. Mrs. Murray observed Horace with Elsie — how carefully he watched over his little girl's recovery, how he managed her diet and exercise, never allowing Elsie to become overly tired or to endanger her still fragile health. The little Scotswoman saw Horace as the most patient and earnest of teachers, honoring his daughter's good mind by encouraging her to learn as much as she could of science and history and the arts. And from her first night at The Oaks, when she participated in the household's evening worship, Mrs. Murray was convinced that Horace had indeed taken God into his heart.

The two adults had many long talks together during Mrs. Murray's visit. She had a fondness for a cup of hot chocolate before bed, and many nights, after Elsie had said her prayers and been tucked in, Horace would join Mrs.

Murray, talking for an hour or so before the blazing fire in the parlor. Naturally, their favorite topic was Elsie, for Horace wanted to learn every detail of his child's early years, and Mrs. Murray was equally curious about the father's plans for Elsie's future.

One evening Horace allowed Elsie to stay up half an hour past her bedtime to finish a book she was reading. Later, as he sat with Mrs. Murray, Horace said in a most thoughtful way, "When we lived at Roselands, my sister Adelaide often chastised me for being too severe with Elsie and expecting perfection from a child. Adelaide's words always made me angry because I judged myself to be the best master of my own daughter. I know now that Adelaide was right and that my behavior was tyrannical."

Mrs. Murray only nodded and sipped her chocolate drink. She sensed that Horace was troubled about something, and she could wait for him to make his point.

"I was so determined that she be *better* than other children," he continued, "that I failed to see how *good* she is. You see, Mrs. Murray, I was brought up with very little discipline, and while I didn't fall victim to the many vices that are the downfall of other boys, I grew headstrong and willful."

"I remember," Mrs. Murray said gently.

"When I came back to Roselands to reclaim Elsie," Horace went on, "I observed the behavior of my half-brothers and half-sisters, and except for Adelaide and Lora, who are the eldest, they all seemed to some degree affected with the same self-centered stubbornness. My brother Arthur has become a cruel and spiteful boy, given to deception and lies. My baby sister Enna is pampered and spoiled in every way."

"They have not, I believe, been trained in the ways of the Lord," Mrs. Murray commented.

"No," Horace replied. "My father is a good and moral man, but his religion has always been for show, as was mine. We went to church and read the Bible, but we never welcomed God into our lives. At any rate, I saw the consequences of lax discipline in my own family, and I was determined that Elsie should be reared differently. But what I considered to be reasonable discipline was as cruel as anything Arthur ever did. I understand that now, and I think I shall always grieve the harshness and coldness I showed my dear loving child."

"Aye," Mrs. Murray agreed. "But you have changed, Mr. Dinsmore, and our Lord is guiding your steps now. I must tell you that I've never seen a more loving and caring father. Your dear, dead wife would be proud of you, I know."

A wistful smile played on Horace's lips, and he said, so softly that Mrs. Murray could barely catch his words, "I hope that is true."

"But I believe, sir, you are worrying that in your new relationship with wee Elsie, you may become too soft with her," Mrs. Murray said in the no-nonsense manner that Horace so enjoyed. "Tonight, for instance, you gave into her wishes and let her stay up when she should have been sent to bed."

"That's exactly it," Horace exclaimed. "Tonight was just a trifling matter, but I so want to make up for my past that I'm inclined to indulge rather than discipline her."

"And that would be a mistake, for every child needs proper discipline," Mrs. Murray said. "The Bible gives you clear instructions, sir. 'Train a child in the way he should go, and when he is old he will not turn from it.' And 'Fathers, do not exasperate your children; instead, bring them up in the training and instruction of the Lord.' God has given you the example, dear man. True love is never blind and indulgent.

"Elsie is but a young thing yet, Mr. Dinsmore, and she needs your love *and* your discipline. There is much for her to learn before she becomes a woman, and I'm convinced that you are her best earthly guide. And when you are unsure of yourself, as all parents sometimes are, turn to your Heavenly Father, and He will show you the way."

"And do you think Elsie will understand when I discipline her?" Horace asked.

"No, not always and not until she is fully grown. But because she's sure of your love, she will trust you and trust that what you do is for her benefit. When you were harsh with her in the past, it was not from mean-spiritedness. I believe you always loved that child more than you ever knew. But even parents need a higher teacher, and your teacher is our precious Lord. Put your faith in Him always, Mr. Dinsmore. Do as He commands. That is how you will know the right and good thing to do."

Horace rose from his chair and came to stand before the little lady. He bent and took her small, thin hand between both of his.

"I hope you will indulge me this once," he said with a warm smile. "I know that you value plain speaking, so I will say plainly that I am and always shall be thankful that it was you who took my child to your heart when her mother died. I was too young and selfish to be a good father then. God gave me a treasure in Elsie, but I did not value the gift. You and Aunt Chloe preserved and protected that treasure for me, and whatever Elsie does in her life, it will be due in large measure to your love and devotion. I am, Mrs. Murray, eternally in your debt."

Horace released her hand and turned toward the fire, which had burned down to embers. He didn't see the solitary tear of joy that rolled down Mrs. Murray's wrinkled cheek.

CHAPTER

2

A Merry Gathering

*"Great is the Lord and most worthy of praise;
His greatness no one can fathom. One
generation will commend your works
to another.... They will celebrate
your abundant goodness and
joyfully sing of your
righteousness."*
PSALM 145:3-4,7

*D*o you think I can finish these in time?" Elsie asked anxiously.

She sat on her four-poster bed and bent her head over a small hoop with which she was working on a crisp square of the whitest linen. On the nearby couch, both Mrs. Murray and Aunt Chloe were busy with their own sewing chores.

"I'm sure you shall," Mrs. Murray said. "You've already completed eight of those handkerchiefs, and I see that you're nearly done with the ninth. That will leave only three to do, and we still have several weeks before Christmas."

"And if you need a little help, darling, Mrs. Murray and I can do a bit of stitching for you," Aunt Chloe added.

"But these handkerchiefs are for Papa's Christmas, so I must do them all myself," Elsie insisted peevishly.

"Nay, bonnie girl," Mrs. Murray said. "Remember that the Apostle Paul spoke of 'those able to help others.' It is important that we put pride aside and accept help when we need it, so that we may give help when it is needed by others."

Elsie was quiet for a few moments. "I never thought of that before," she said at last, "but you're right, dear Mrs. Murray. I'm making these handkerchiefs for my Papa, and if I need your help to finish them, I should be glad to ask for it. Oh, Mrs. Murray, I'm so happy that you are here to explain things to me. With you and Papa and Aunt Chloe, I have so many good teachers."

"That's mighty true," Aunt Chloe said brightly. "Having Mrs. Murray with us here — it's like old times."

Elsie had returned to her embroidery and was carefully drawing her needle and silk thread through the intricately

17

outlined "D" she was monogramming on the cloth. Without looking up, she said, "I hope you can stay with us always, Mrs. Murray."

The old lady merely commented, "Thank you, dear bairn," but Aunt Chloe caught the shadow that passed over Mrs. Murray's thin face. The nursemaid knew what Elsie did not — that Mrs. Murray would be returning to her native land before spring arrived.

"Have you and your father decided what you will be doing for Christmas?" Mrs. Murray asked, changing the subject. "I know you have an invitation to spend the season with the Howards, and I'm sure you'd like to see your friend Carrie."

"I would indeed," Elsie replied with feeling, "But Papa says the Howards' house party will be very large. You remember Christmas at Roselands last year, Aunt Chloe?"

"I do, I do," Chloe said, laughing. "It was a mighty fine party, sure enough, and a powerful lot of work for the servants with all those folks to tend to. Old Aunt Phoebe seemed to be at her stove day and night, and Pompey — why, I'd never seen that man move so fast, and still he couldn't get everything done for everybody! He and Jim near about wore out that road to the city, riding back and forth on errands for all those guests."

"It was fun to see so many friends at once," Elsie remarked, "but I told Papa that I'd like a quiet Christmas this year, and he said that was what he wanted as well. He said that we should start our own Christmas day tradition at The Oaks and that I could decide whom to invite."

"And who will that be?" Mrs. Murray inquired.

"I've been thinking about it." Elsie paused in her work. "Grandpa and Mrs. Dinsmore and most of the children will be going to the Howards. But I think Aunt Adelaide would like to join us, and maybe Lora, too. Lora has never enjoyed big parties the way Louise and Enna do. And we'll invite Mr. Travilla, of course, and his mother and Doctor Barton if he can come. They were all so kind to me when I was sick."

"That will make a merry party," Mrs. Murray said.

A little shyly, Elsie went on, "Papa would be very honored, Mrs. Murray, if you would be hostess for the day. He says that when I'm older, I'll be his hostess, and I can learn from you. Will you do it, please, Mrs. Murray? It would make me — and Papa, of course — so happy."

Mrs. Murray's dark eyes had widened with delighted surprise. "Why, it would be my honor, dear child. And you will be my assistant with all the preparations."

"And Aunt Chloe," Elsie continued, "Papa wants all the servants to have a wonderful party. He says that Christmas should be a day of joyful celebration for everyone, because it is Jesus' birthday. Will you plan the servants' party, Aunt Chloe? Papa says that Jim can help you with everything you need."

Now it was Chloe's turn to beam. "Sure enough, Elsie darling, I'll do it up right. But does Mister Horace mean house servants and field hands, too?"

"Oh, yes, Aunt Chloe. He says that the day of our Lord's birth is for everyone. As soon as Papa returns this afternoon, I'll tell him you both agree." Elsie's face fairly glowed with happiness, and both women noticed how healthy the little girl looked.

"This is going to be a wonderful Christmas," Elsie exclaimed, then quickly she bent back to her little hoop and added, "if I get these handkerchiefs done in time!"

Elsie's New Life

The next few weeks bustled with activity at The Oaks. Even a small Christmas demanded large efforts, and Elsie, who was allowed to help both Mrs. Murray and Aunt Chloe, saw for the first time how much work was really required. Not that anyone resented the extra chores; on the contrary, everyone looked forward to the day when the entire population of The Oaks would remember, in grateful prayers and celebrations, God's gift to His children of His "only begotten Son."

Horace gave Elsie a sum of money for Christmas shopping, in addition to her monthly allowance, and she and Mrs. Murray spent a number of pleasant afternoons in the city, purchasing gifts for one and all. Elsie selected special items for all her family at Roselands, from her grandfather to little Enna. She even bought a present for Arthur, who was to stay at his boarding school throughout the holidays — a copy of Bunyan's *Pilgrim's Progress*. She choose an elegant purse in gold and silver beading for her Aunt Adelaide, and a beautiful silk scarf in shades of blue that would highlight Lora's lovely eyes. She bought a handsome, small, leather-bound book of prayers for Mrs. Travilla, and in the same book shop, she found a small engraving of English garden flowers for Edward Travilla. She was uncertain what to get for Doctor Barton, but at Mrs. Murray's suggestion, she at last selected an ebony writing pen "to match his black bag." She also helped Mrs. Murray pick out gifts for all the servants, from eldest to youngest. For Aunt Chloe, Elsie chose a robe of the warmest, softest wool with slippers to match. Her gift to Mrs. Murray, bought by her father so as to keep it secret, was a beautiful new Bible, bound in leather and edged in gold.

Horace was caught up in the Christmas spirit as much as Elsie, but he was ever-watchful of her health and education. He continued her morning lessons, with emphasis on the geography of the Holy Land, where he had visited once during his years abroad. Elsie was fascinated with his recollections of the places where Jesus had lived and taught, especially Jerusalem and Galilee.

Since her illness, father and daughter had fallen into the habit of reading aloud to each other in the evening. Elsie's favorite stories were the historical novels of Sir Walter Scott, a Scottish writer of whom Horace thoroughly approved. Now, they often asked Mrs. Murray to join them, and she quickly became their favorite reader — her rich accent (which Mrs. Murray called her "burr") adding to the thrilling tales of *Rob Roy* and *Ivanhoe* and *Quentin Durward*.

One afternoon, not many days before Christmas, Elsie and Horace were in the library when John came to the door and announced the arrival of a business associate of Horace.

"I will meet with him in the parlor," Horace instructed. "Tell him I will be there in a few minutes."

As John went to see to the guest, Horace gathered together the letters he had been writing and glanced at Elsie, who was curled up in a large leather chair and so engrossed in a book that she hadn't noticed John's interruption.

"Elsie, dear," Horace said, "I have a business meeting to attend. It shouldn't take too long, but the afternoon is waning, and I want you to have your walk before it grows dark. You may read for fifteen minutes more. If I have not returned by then, go and get Aunt Chloe to walk with you."

"I will, Papa," Elsie promised, "but I wish I could read longer."

"That book will be here when you return, but you need the fresh air. What is it that so commands your attention?"

Her eyes sparkling with excitement, Elsie said. "It is Scott's *Lady of the Lake*, Papa. It's so good, and I never knew before that a poem could also be such a grand adventure."

Horace smiled: "Indeed, Elsie, poetry is an adventure. But mind what I say. Fifteen minutes, then take your walk. And be sure to dress warmly."

"Yes, sir."

Horace's meeting was much lengthier than he had anticipated, and when his business friend finally departed, the winter evening had turned dark. Returning to the library, Horace was surprised to see Elsie there in almost exactly the same position as he had left her.

He came to her side and gently lifted the book from her hands. Elsie looked up with a start, and even in the firelight, Horace could see the blush that flooded her cheeks. She had been so absorbed in her book that she was totally unaware of the time, but the stern look on Horace's face told her that something was terribly amiss.

"It has been almost two hours since I left," Horace said in the serious voice Elsie had not heard for so long, "and I can see that you have not stirred from this chair. Elsie, you have disobeyed me and broken your promise."

"Oh, Papa," she cried in real dismay, "I didn't mean to. I was reading and I never thought . . . Are you going to punish me?"

"Yes, dear, but let's talk about it first," Horace said, a little smile tugging at his lips. He lifted Elsie gently from the chair and then took her place, settling her beside him and wrapping his arm around her.

In a small, trembling voice, Elsie said, "I'm so sorry I disobeyed, Papa. I didn't intend to, but I know that's no excuse. Can you forgive me?"

"Of course, I forgive you, but I must punish you as well so that you will remember the importance of obedience. I will take the book from you for a week, and I believe that will be an adequate lesson."

"Thank you, Papa," Elsie said softly. "I deserve worse, for I was very disobedient. I don't deserve your being so forgiving."

"I want you to understand, Elsie, that your punishment is for your disobedience in this matter only. You have my forgiveness whether it is deserved or not — just as our Heavenly Father forgives us and offers us His full and free pardon without consideration of what we deserve. As the Apostle Peter tells us, 'everyone who believes in Him receives forgiveness of sins through His name.'"

Horace went on, speaking aloud but in a musing tone, "I have been too free with my punishments in the past, but God has taught me the true meaning of forgiveness. I shall never punish you from any feeling of revenge or because I think you have somehow slighted me, dearest child. Yes, it disappoints me when you disobey, but my punishment is intended to teach you, never to harm or hurt you. I have selected a punishment that fits your deed."

He gave her a little hug and held her closer. "You know that I love you more than anything in all the world, but because I love you, I don't intend to spoil you. Spoiling you would be a cruelty, and selfishness on my part. Trust me, Elsie, I shall never again ask you to go against your conscience or disobey our Heavenly Father's commands. But I still expect your obedience, and your duty is to obey me. Do you understand?"

"Yes, Papa," Elsie replied. "But it's hard sometimes not to want to have my own way."

"That's true for us all, child and adult," Horace said. "We must ask God to help us give up our willfulness and to be satisfied with what we *ought* to do, rather than what we *want* to do. You will learn, dear, as I've learned, that doing what we *ought* brings us the truest happiness."

"I know you're right, Papa, and I'll try very hard."

And so, while the rest of the house busied itself with cooking and cleaning and the myriad preparations for the approaching holiday, Horace and his daughter passed the half hour before the supper bell rang in peaceful silence, each one considering in their own fashion the meanings of duty and forgiveness.

Elsie was up and dressed so early on Christmas morning that her father was still completing his attire when she knocked at his door. She was wearing a white pinafore over a lovely pink dress that enhanced the glow of her cheeks and the luster of her brown curls. "Merry Christmas, Papa!" she exclaimed, rushing to his open arms.

Horace had not seen her looking so completely well for many, many months, and as her lifted her for a hug, he offered up a silent prayer of thanks for her restoration.

Seeing that her father still wore his robe over his clothes, Elsie said with a giggle, "You haven't finished dressing, Papa. Perhaps I can help you."

It was then Horace noticed the square bundle in her hand, a packet wrapped in shiny white paper and tied with a red ribbon. Setting Elsie on the floor, Horace took the package she offered, and untied the ribbon. Opening the paper, he saw a neat stack of white, linen handkerchiefs, each one neatly embroidered in one corner with his own handsomely designed initial.

"Is this your work?" he asked as he thumbed through the stack. "All twelve of them?"

Elsie nodded, hoping her gift pleased him.

"They are beautifully done," he said with a broad smile. "Why your needlework is as skillful as any I have seen in Paris or London."

Elsie flushed with pleasure. "You can carry one today, Papa," she suggested.

"I will, with pride. And you have provided me with enough handkerchiefs so I can carry one every day. Thank you, dearest, for giving me a gift of your own making; it means all the more to me that they come from your handiwork. But whenever did you find the time?"

Elsie ducked her head. Softly she said, "I started them last spring, Papa, while you were away. I wanted to give them to you when you returned, but then I got sick."

Horace dropped to one knee and cradled her against his shoulder. "Oh, I am so sorry, Elsie, so sorry for that time."

"But, Papa," Elsie said, surprised at his sadness. "I was able to finish them here, at The Oaks, with a little help from Aunt Chloe. So I didn't think of Roselands when I worked on them. I thought of my new home with you."

"And so shall I," Horace said a little hoarsely. Hurriedly, he got to his feet again and went to his bedside table, taking a small box from the drawer.

"Now, it's my turn to give," he said. He opened the box, revealing a glistening pearl necklace and two matching bracelets. He put the pearls around her neck, securing the clasp, and then stood back.

"They're beautiful, Papa, and so grown up," Elsie cried delightedly.

"Not too grown up," Horace laughed. Thinking suddenly of the years he had deprived himself of Elsie's presence in his life, he added a little wistfully, "We have some years yet, I hope, before my daughter is too grown up."

After breakfast and the household's morning worship, Elsie helped her father distribute a large stack of gifts to the house servants, and when each gift had been opened and admired, Horace excused himself and Elsie. There were more gifts to be delivered to the quarters where the field hands and their families lived. It was a clear, crisp morning, and Elsie could smell the fires and the aromas of good cooking before the heavy-laden cart reached the enclave of slave cabins.

When Horace and Elsie returned to the house, it was approaching time for the arrival of their guests. In fact, Edward Travilla rode up just a few minutes later. His mother in her carriage was stopping by Roselands to pick up Adelaide. (Lora had not been able to accept Horace's invitation. At her mother's insistence, she had gone to the Howards' house party instead, but she had expressed her disappointment in a sweet note to Elsie several days earlier.) Mrs. Murray greeted each guest while Horace freshened up and Aunt Chloe quickly brushed Elsie's hair and changed her into her white lace party dress with the green satin sash.

By one o'clock everyone was in the drawing room save Doctor Barton. A tall pine tree, decorated by Mrs. Murray and Elsie with bows of brightly colored ribbons and clusters of holly berries and mistletoe, stood in front of the glass doors and glowed in the sunlight. Arrangements of pine and holly stood on the mantle, and the whole room was bright with Christmas and the companionship of good friends. Mrs. Murray and Mrs. Travilla had a grand conversation about Scotland, which Mrs. Travilla had visited when Edward was but a boy. Adelaide and Elsie chatted about many things, including Elsie's reading of Sir Walter Scott, whose works were so popular in Southern homes. Horace and Edward talked of politics for awhile, then Edward asked, "Is Adelaide to serve as your hostess today, or have you appointed Elsie to that post?"

"I shall give Elsie a few more years for that," Horace replied, a faraway look coming into his eyes. "No, I have asked Mrs. Murray to take the head of the table today, for she was closest to the lady whose place is rightly there - my wife. And I have developed the deepest respect for our Scottish guest. She is a woman of great insight and virtue, and she's been of much assistance to me over the past two months."

"Have you thought of asking her to stay?" Edward asked.

Horace lowered his voice. "Not only thought, but done," he said. "I've offered her the position of housekeeper and companion to Elsie, for as long as she likes, but alas, she cannot accept."

"But why? She seems quite at home here, and her devotion to Elsie is plain enough."

"Mrs. Murray has responsibilities in Scotland that she cannot shirk. Two orphaned great-nieces, not much older than Elsie, require her love and attention there, so she must go back in another month."

Horace put his hand on Edward's arm and bent closer. "Say nothing of it, friend, for I haven't told Elsie yet. I wanted this Christmas to be free from all clouds for her."

Edward nodded his assent. Then he said mischievously, "So who will be your hostess next year? You cannot find substitutes every season until Elsie is grown. Isn't it about time this house of yours had a permanent mistress?"

Horace actually blushed behind his beard and replied shortly, "Isn't that remark better suited to someone who does not live in a glass house. It seems to me, Edward, that you are the true bachelor in this room."

Edward laughed heartily, attracting Elsie's attention. Noting her look, he said playfully, "Oh, I will wait for Elsie to be my hostess."

The hour wore on in pleasantries, and it was only as a servant came to announce dinner that Doctor Barton hurried in. His coat was dusty and his hair tousled, and he wore a huge grin.

"I apologize for my lateness," he said breathlessly, "but I have just been delivering a Christmas present."

"What was it that required such a last-minute rush?" Horace asked.

"A baby boy," the doctor laughed. "A bouncing baby boy delivered to one of your neighbors just in time for Christmas!"

Christmas dinner was a long and delicious affair, with five courses in all including the most wonderful selection of desserts Elsie had ever seen. When she was asked which she would choose — the many-layered cake with coconut icing or the rich cream custard or the brightly colored fruit trifle which was Mrs. Murray's recipe, or any of several more — she looked doubtfully at her father, for she knew well his rule that she not eat sweets without his permission. Horace smiled and said, "Today, the choice is yours, Daughter. The cook and Mrs. Murray have planned this excellent meal for us, and you should enjoy the ending of it as well as the beginning. Tomorrow is time enough for stewed fruit." So Elsie asked for Mrs. Murray's trifle and enjoyed every bit.

After their feast, the party gathered again in the drawing room to exchange gifts. Each and every one received as they gave, with courtesy and much good fun. Elsie was particularly pleased with a new Bible, inscribed with her name, from Aunt Adelaide. It was a happy group that parted company as night fell. As dinner was so late, no supper was served that night, though Mrs. Murray prepared hot chocolate and plain biscuits for Elsie.

There was, however, one more gift to be exchanged. When Elsie was in bed, her father came to her room for their nightly Scripture reading and prayer. Elsie chose the second chapter of Luke for the simple story of Jesus' birth and the glorious "good news of great joy." When he had finished reading, Horace remarked, "It's good to read these verses again, to remind ourselves of the true meaning of Christmas."

"Yes, Papa," Elsie said thoughtfully. "I love my new necklace and bracelets and all the nice things everyone gave me, but the real gift is from God, isn't it?"

"It is indeed, dearest — the gift of salvation," Horace said earnestly. "Now, Elsie, I have a request to make of you. Your aunt gave you a beautiful new Bible today."

"Yes, Papa. Wasn't that a thoughtful gift?"

"It certainly was. And since you cannot use two Bibles at once, would you be willing to give your old one to me?"

Elsie didn't reply at once. For a moment, her brow wrinkled with doubt, but then she smiled gently and said, "I wouldn't part with it for anyone else. It's very worn, I know, but it was my Mamma's, and it has been with me through so many troubles. But I'd be very happy to give it to you, Papa."

Horace wrapped her in a warm embrace. "And I am very grateful," he said, "because your little Bible sustained me too, through a time when I imagined that I had lost what I value most in all this world. Thank you, dearest, for your generous heart. I will cherish this special book."

CHAPTER

3

Two Departures

"'For I know the plans I have for you,'
declares the Lord, 'plans to prosper
you and not to harm you, plans
to give you hope and
a future.'"
JEREMIAH 29:11

Two Departures

everal days after the New Year, Horace told Elsie about Mrs. Murray's plans to return to Scotland. He anticipated tears, and was most surprised by his daughter's reaction. Elsie was naturally sad to learn that her old friend would be leaving The Oaks at month's end, but she did not cry or grieve as Horace expected.

"I'm sorry she can't stay with us," Elsie said. "But she has told me all about her nieces and how they lost their mamma and papa in a terrible accident. They need her now, just as I needed her when my Mamma died."

"You are being uncommonly understanding," Horace commented. "I must admit that I expected you to be very upset."

"Well, I would have been," Elsie said slowly, "if I didn't have you to love me and take care of me. I remember all those years when you were away, and I am so lucky that my Papa returned to me. But that can't happen for Mrs. Murray's nieces. Both their parents have gone to God, and without Mrs. Murray, they would be alone. So I can be happy that she is going back to them, even though I'm sad she is leaving us. It's strange, isn't it, Papa, how a person can feel two ways at the same time — sad, but also happy."

"It is a very grown-up feeling," Horace said softly.

Together, Elsie and Horace resolved to make Mrs. Murray's last month at The Oaks as special as they could. Horace planned several trips into the city — once to attend a play — and visits to the Travillas at Ion. (Mrs. Travilla and Mrs. Murray had struck up quite a friendship, for both ladies were deeply committed Christians who also shared a fondness for lively conversation.) Mrs. Murray seemed to take a special liking to Edward Travilla after he escorted her on a tour of his hothouse, which bloomed like an oasis in the dead of winter.

As the date of Mrs. Murray's departure approached, however, a quietness seemed to settle over The Oaks. It was a difficult time for everyone: Aunt Chloe hated the thought of parting with her old friend, and Horace with his new one. Mrs. Murray, who had answered Horace's invitation in order to see for herself that Elsie was safe and sound, had found herself welcomed so warmly at The Oaks that she now felt as if she were leaving her own family. And Elsie — poor Elsie worked very hard to keep up a brave front, but her little heart was breaking at the thought that she might never see Mrs. Murray again. Scotland was so very far away, and to Elsie's ten-year-old eyes, Mrs. Murray seemed so very old and frail.

One morning, after their devotion, Elsie spoke about her fears to her father. "Am I being very selfish," she asked, "to wish Mrs. Murray could stay with us?"

"Your feeling is very human," Horace replied kindly. "I know that you want Mrs. Murray to do what is right and to return to her home and her young nieces. But it is natural that you shall miss her. I think you should take this problem to our Heavenly Father. He can take the weight from your heart."

Elsie did just that, and through prayer, her heart was lightened. She understood that distance would not diminish her love for Mrs. Murray, nor Mrs. Murray's love for her. Whether they met again was in God's hands, and Elsie put all her trust in Him.

When the hour of parting arrived, it was accomplished with as many smiles as tears. Aunt Chloe dabbed at her eyes and presented her friend with a splendid hand-crocheted shawl to keep her warm on the long ocean voyage. Mrs. Travilla and Edward had come to The Oaks to bid their farewells, and gave Mrs. Murray one of Edward's most fragrant potted plants to brighten her ship's cabin. Elsie's gift was a simple but elegant silver ring that had once belonged to her mother, and the little girl promised to write her friend faithfully.

Horace's present was to come later, for unknown to Mrs. Murray, he had established a bank account in Edinburgh which would provide her with a generous, lifelong income as well as an inheritance for her nieces. But as he helped Mrs. Murray into the carriage at The Oaks, he simply said to her, "I cannot predict the future, dear lady, for that is the province of our Lord, but I can tell you how important you have become to me in the present. No one could have been a better friend to my child, and I am honored by your friendship now. I shall cherish the hope that we will all meet again in this life, if it is God's will."

As the carriage disappeared down the driveway, Horace saw that Elsie was trembling, and he quickly led her inside, out of the windy cold.

Spring comes early in the South, and by mid-March, the fields around The Oaks were turning to green again, dotted here and there with masses of early daffodils and banded by ribbons of yellow forsythia hedge. The bare trees seemed highlighted in red as their branches began to bud. Flocks of geese formed V's in the clear skies, making their flights northward from the marshlands. The whole world appeared to be renewing itself as the earth and the air warmed.

Elsie's New Life

Horace, however, was growing increasingly concerned. As March became April, and the gardens burst into color, Elsie seemed to be losing her strength. She tired more easily than she had since the previous summer, and on one of her afternoon rides with her father, her face suddenly turned a deathly pale, and she felt so dizzy that Horace lifted her into his arms and carried her home on his horse.

At first, Doctor Barton prescribed a change in diet, but when Elsie grew more lethargic, the doctor spoke frankly to her father. "I do not think this is dangerous," he assured Horace, "but Elsie has never fully recovered from her fever, and the heat of the coming summer can do her no good. Is it possible to take her to a cooler climate for the hot months?"

Horace replied, "I had already planned to take Elsie for a summer holiday, but do you think we should go now?"

"I do. We seem to be in for an unseasonable spring, so the sooner the better. Can you afford to leave at present?"

"Will two weeks from now be soon enough? I have just hired a very good man to manage The Oaks in my absence, but I had not expected him to begin work for another month. I'm sure he can come early, but I will need a little time to train him."

"Two or three weeks should be fine. Just be sure she takes this tonic I'm prescribing and keep her on the new diet. You get your business in order so you can enjoy your travels. Where do you plan to go?"

Horace thought for a moment. "You know, old friend," he said, "I think I shall give the choice of destinations to my daughter."

When Doctor Barton had gone, Horace went to Elsie's sitting room where she was working on her lessons for the day.

She looked up as he entered. "Is it time already, Papa?" she asked. "I'm not quite sure of this passage yet."

"Look at your clock dear, and you will see that I am early. I have some news for you, and I need your help."

"Is it good news, Papa?"

"I hope you will think so," he replied, settling into a comfortable chair. "I've decided to take you to the North for the summer, and I plan that we should leave in about two weeks' time. Doctor Barton thinks that the cooler climate will be just the thing to restore your health. Aunt Chloe and John will accompany us, but I need your help deciding where we should go."

"Really, Papa?" Elsie exclaimed. Clapping her hands with delight when Horace nodded his assent, she said, "Can we visit Miss Rose, Papa, in Philadelphia? I so want to see her again, and I know you will like her very much."

"Of course we may go to Philadelphia, dearest," he agreed. "I will be happy to meet your Miss Allison. And there is much to see and do in Philadelphia besides. Where else would you like to go? Take your pencil and paper, and we will make a list."

"Well," Elsie began thoughtfully, "I think I'd like to visit all the places I've learned about in history. There's Washington, of course. Oh, it would be so interesting to see the Capitol and the President's house. And New York, and Boston." She was scribbling rapidly, trying to make her pencil keep up with the pace of her ideas. "I'd so like to go to Bunker Hill and see where our Revolution began — Papa, did you really mean *wherever* I want to go?"

"That's what I said, and you know I am a man of my word," Horace responded, laughing aloud at her enthusiasm.

"Then I'd like to see the Great Lakes, Champlain and Ontario, and Niagara Falls. And maybe we could sail on the Hudson River and the Connecticut River and visit the White Mountains." She worked at her list, then scratched her head. "I can't think of any more right now, Papa."

"I would say you have made a very good beginning. This will occupy us for quite some time. I can see that I have a number of arrangements to make," Horace said with a broad smile.

"Because I will be so busy the next two weeks, what do you say we forgo some of your lessons?" he asked. Elsie's face immediately fell, so he quickly explained, "You will continue your music and drawing lessons with your tutors, and you and I will concentrate on history lessons about the places we are to visit. That and your packing should keep you occupied."

"Yes, Papa, that's an excellent plan," Elsie said, her face beaming once more. "May I write to Miss Allison now and tell her we are coming?"

"Not quite yet, dear. From your list, I believe we should visit Washington first, before it is too warm there. That is when you should write to Miss Allison."

Elsie rose from her desk and went to give her father a loving hug. "Thank you so much, Papa," she said, planting a warm kiss on his cheek. "This will be a wonderful trip, just like our first summer together when you took me to such nice places."

"I think you enjoy traveling," Horace said, returning her hug. "In that we are very much alike."

Horace did look forward to the trip, almost as much as Elsie, though he felt a small regret at missing his first full growing season at The Oaks. But the plantation manager he had hired was a competent man, and Horace's father readily agreed to keep an eye on the farm until Horace's return. In truth, the senior Mr. Dinsmore welcomed this opportunity to assist his son and granddaughter, for he deeply regretted his own part in the poor treatment Elsie had received at Roselands and had sought a means to make some amends.

Elsie could talk of little else but the trip during the next two weeks, and Horace believed he could see already some improvement in her condition. On the day they departed, taking the carriage into the city where they would board a train for the North, Elsie could barely contain her excitement. At the last moment, however, as she looked back from the carriage window at the plantation house, now framed in spring green, she felt a little tug in her chest at leaving her lovely home behind. She reached for her father's hand, and was reassured by his gentle squeeze.

CHAPTER

A Northern Adventure

*"Now may our God and Father
Himself and our Lord
Jesus clear the way for
us to come to you."*

1 Thessalonians 3:11

ashington was an exciting, if dusty, young city. Many of the streets were still dirt roads, which could turn into rivers of mud in a spring rain. There were new buildings being constructed everywhere, and Elsie thought it a good thing that she was accustomed to waking early, for not even their hotel walls could keep out the sounds of hammering and sawing that began as soon as the sun rose each day.

At Elsie's request, they visited first the Capitol where the Congress met and then the house of the President. The President's home was grand, though not so large as she expected; in her mind's eye, Elsie had envisioned a palace, but her father explained that the United States was a democracy in which the President lived in a house like everyone else. Horace told her that the site of the house was selected by George Washington himself, though the first President never lived there. Elsie was fascinated when Horace recounted how the British had burned the place to its stone walls during the War of 1812 and how the President's wife, Mrs. Madison, had saved the portrait of George Washington from the flames.

They spent several days in Baltimore where Horace had friends, and Elsie was amazed by the many tall ships in the harbor there. Horace pointed out one that he said was just like the ship in which he had sailed home to her from Europe.

"Is it wonderful to be on the ocean, Papa?" she asked.

"It can be," he replied, remembering his last, rough, early spring crossing. "It can also be very frightening when there is a storm."

"But God is always watching over you, Papa. You need-n't be afraid when God is protecting you."

"I did not know God's love so well back then," Horace mused.

From Baltimore, they traveled back to Washington by way of Annapolis where Elsie saw more ships, as well as colonial houses that had been built long before the United States became a nation.

"There's history everywhere we look, isn't there, Papa?" Elsie asked as they strolled a walkway beside the Chesapeake River.

"That's true, my dear, just as history is being made every day."

They stayed more than two weeks in Washington and Maryland, and it was the first week of May when Chloe and John began packing everyone's cases and Horace purchased train tickets. Though Elsie enjoyed all the sights that the capital city had to offer, she had become anxious to move on, for their next destination was Philadelphia and that meant the happiest of reunions with Miss Allison.

Rose Allison, a young woman just a year older than Elsie's Aunt Adelaide, was the best friend Elsie had made at Roselands. It had happened several years earlier, just before Horace's return, when Rose was visiting with the Dinsmores for a winter. On meeting Elsie, Rose had seen in the little girl a kindred spirit, for Rose was, like Elsie, a dedicated Christian. Rose had also seen how unfairly the child was treated by others in the family, and she had brought the light of kindness into little Elsie's lonely life. Rose remained the truest of friends, writing at least once each month since returning to her own family and offering Elsie the wisest of counsel in the child's most troubled times.

Elsie could hardly wait to look into Rose's gentle face once again. She had written Rose a letter, included with Horace's letter to Rose's father — a close friend of the elder Mr. Dinsmore — and posted it a few days before their departure from Washington.

When their train arrived in Philadelphia, Elsie entreated her father to go straightway to the Allison's town house, for she could not wait a minute more. Horace demurred: "But to descend upon friends without warning — Elsie, that would be a grave discourtesy. Besides, you are looking somewhat tired. We'll go to our hotel, and Aunt Chloe can give you a warm bath, and then you can have your supper and get to bed early."

"But, Papa —"

"No 'but's'. While Aunt Chloe cares for you, I will send John to deliver our calling cards to the Allisons. We will probably hear from them by tomorrow, and then you can meet Miss Allison when you are rested from a good night's sleep."

Elsie knew better than to protest further, and she was feeling tired from the train ride. In fact, once they had settled into their hotel suite and Elsie had bathed, been dressed in her nightclothes and warm robe by Aunt Chloe, and eaten a delicious supper delivered to her room, she could barely keep her eyes open. Horace sat with her while she ate, and when the meal was done, he asked if she would like to hear a story from one of the new books she had bought in Washington.

"No, thank you, Papa. Will you read from my Bible instead? I'm afraid I may fall asleep before our prayers if I have a story."

Horace chose the first chapter of the Book of Ruth, which recounts the love and loyalty of Ruth to her mother-in-law, Naomi. After they had completed their prayers, Elsie climbed into the large feather bed, and Horace pulled the covers close under her chin.

"Sleep well, my Daughter," he said, bending to kiss her forehead.

"Maybe Miss Rose will call on us in the morning," Elsie said sleepily.

"We shall see," Horace replied as he turned out the oil lamp on the bedside table.

By eight o'clock the next morning, Elsie was already growing nervous and excited.

"When will she come, Papa? Will it be soon?"

"It's too early for anyone to call," Horace said kindly. "You must learn patience, my dear. We don't know if the Allisons have even received our cards yet. I'll tell you what we shall do. We'll have our breakfast and then read from that guidebook about Philadelphia until ten o'clock. Then I will go down to the hotel desk and check to see if we have received any messages. If we haven't heard from the Allisons by then, I'll take you to see Independence Hall."

"But we may miss her if we leave the hotel, Papa! Can't we just stay at the hotel till she calls on us?" Elsie pleaded.

Horace, thinking that a message would likely arrive from Miss Allison or her father, was inclined to be indulgent. "Very well," he said. "We will stay here until after our dinner. But if there is no word by then, we'll go out and see some of the sights."

Elsie started to say something, but Horace anticipated her remarks. "And if Miss Allison calls while we are away,

she will leave her card, and we'll go to see her immediately. But neither you nor I will benefit from staying in these hotel rooms day and night."

When there was no message from the Allisons after dinner that day, Horace firmly instructed Elsie to don her spring coat and bonnet, for it was a cool day, and join him for a walk. At first she was distracted, looking not at the historic city but at every young woman who bore the slightest resemblance to Rose Allison. But gradually her attention was drawn to the sites where her country was born. Her father regaled her with stories of the Founding Fathers — how they gathered for the First Continental Congress in Carpenters Hall in 1774, then assembled again in the State House, now called Independence Hall, just two years later to create an army and name George Washington as its commander. Horace told her how the Declaration of Independence had been adopted here on a hot July day in 1776 and how the Constitution was framed in the same building in 1787. Inside the Hall, Elsie knew, hung the Liberty Bell, which bore an inscription from the Old Testament: "Proclaim liberty throughout all the land, unto all the inhabitants thereof."

"Can we go inside, Papa," Elsie asked, "and see the Bell?"

"Not today. It's growing late, and I want to get you back to the hotel before the air grows chill. We'll return tomorrow and take a proper tour."

Elsie, remembering that a message from Miss Allison might be awaiting them, agreed, but when they reached the hotel and Horace checked at the desk, there was still no news.

Taking a seat on a couch in the hotel's elegant lobby, Horace drew Elsie beside him and put his arm about her shoulders. "I begin to fear," he said in his gentlest voice, "that Miss Allison and her family are not at home. John told me that their house was closed and unlighted when he delivered our cards last night, so I sent another note this morning. From what I know of the Allisons, they would surely have responded by now if they were in the city. Your grandfather told me that Mr. Allison maintains a summer home somewhere outside the city, and perhaps they are staying there. Unfortunately, I don't have an address."

"Maybe they are just away for a few days," Elsie said hopefully, "and they'll return before we leave Philadelphia."

"Let's hope so, dearest. In the meantime, we will let the City of Brotherly Love entertain us. There is a great deal to be seen here, and we will begin as we planned, with Independence Hall. And on the next day I'll take you to the Academy of Fine Arts. I also have in mind a day or two at Valley Forge. We can travel there by train."

Again Horace proved to be the most attentive of guides and teachers, and Elsie enjoyed each new day of their Pennsylvania visit. The trip to Valley Forge was made especially interesting by an elderly lady whom they met at the old stone building that had been General Washington's headquarters. She invited them inside and gave them a tour of her house, which had belonged to a man named Isaac Potts when the Continental Army camped in the valley. She showed them the small room where the General slept during that winter of 1778, and with great drama, she revealed the hiding place where the General kept his maps and papers.

"It was a bitter winter," the old woman explained as they looked out over the small valley. "The soldiers lived in tents and crude huts and had the barest of supplies. Many of the patriots died of the cold and fevers and disease. But General Washington held his men together, and by spring, new recruits and supplies arrived, and the Army was ready to fight the British."

"General Washington was a remarkable leader," Horace said with admiration in his voice.

"That he was," the old lady responded. "If the Army had broken that winter, I'm not sure we would have a United States today."

Elsie was unusually quiet on the train ride back to Philadelphia, and Horace feared that she had become over-tired by their exertions. He placed his palm on her forehead and was relieved to feel no fever.

"Are you feeling well?" he asked her.

"Yes, Papa," Elsie replied. "I was just thinking of all those men at Valley Forge and what they had to suffer. War is a bad thing, isn't it, Papa?"

"It is, my dear. But those men believed in their cause, and their faith gave them the courage to endure. They fought so that their children and grandchildren could be free."

Elsie looked into her father's face, her hazel eyes dark and serious. "But Papa," she said, "not everyone is free. Aunt Chloe and John and all the servants — they aren't free like you and I. I don't understand, Papa."

Horace hugged her warmly and said, "I don't really understand either. But your question is an important one, and many people of good will are asking the same. I think," he continued, speaking to himself more than his child, "that when your question is resolved, it may be at a very high cost."

"Cost, Papa?" Elsie asked, catching his words. "Do you mean it will cost money?"

"It may, dearest, but I had in mind another kind of cost," Horace said. Then he deliberately changed his expression and went on, "But let's think of other things today. Shall I tell you about General Washington's victory at Trenton and how he crossed the Delaware River?"

———————

They had been in Philadelphia for some ten days, and still no word had come from the Allisons. Over breakfast, Horace said to Elsie, "I am certain now that the Allisons have left this city for the summer, and I think it is time we should also make our departure. Tomorrow is the Sabbath, so I've made arrangements for us to leave on the morning after for New York, then on to Boston. We still have a great many places on your list to see, Elsie."

His little girl bent her head over her plate but said nothing.

"Don't be too disappointed," Horace went on cheerfully, "for I have a plan. We'll continue our travels, going north as the weather warms, to Niagara Falls and the lakes. But we will come back to Philadelphia at summer's end. The Allisons should be returned by then, and we will have a good, long visit with Miss Allison and her family before our journey home to The Oaks."

Elsie looked up. Tears glistened in her bright eyes, but she was smiling. "That's a good plan, Papa, and I will try very hard to be patient," she said.

"Then what would you like to do today?" Horace asked.

Elsie considered. "I think I'd like to visit the Academy of Fine Arts again, Papa. There were several paintings I'd like to see once more."

"Then get your bonnet, and we'll be off to the Academy!" Horace exclaimed heartily.

Elsie and her father had been looking at paintings for about an hour, and Elsie was engrossed in a handsome landscape when she felt a gentle hand on her shoulder.

"Can it be?" a warm voice said just behind her. "Can it be my little friend?"

Elsie spun around and beheld the face she had waited so long to see. Rose Allison! It was like a dream. Rose knelt and embraced Elsie, and Elsie hugged back with all her might, too happy for words.

Behind them, Horace and Rose's companion, a tall young man who appeared a few years older than Rose, looked at one another in some astonishment, for neither had ever seen the other before. Then a slow smile spread on Horace's face.

"Why, this must be the missing Miss Allison," he said.

"It is, Papa! It is my Miss Rose!" Elsie exclaimed.

Rose turned to her companion. "And this is my dear little friend Elsie Dinsmore," she said. Looking back at Elsie's beaming face, Rose asked, "But where did you come from? I had no idea you were in the North."

"We've been in Philadelphia for more than a week, and we tried to find you, but you were gone, and your house was closed," Elsie blurted in a stream of excitement. "And we were going to leave day after tomorrow, and I thought I might never see you!" Elsie hugged Rose again.

"It's a good thing we share an interest in art," Horace said. Then he extended his hand, helping Rose to her feet as he continued, "I am Horace Dinsmore, Jr., father of this most happy child."

"And I am Rose Allison, a friend of your child," Rose said. Then she introduced the young man at her side as her brother, Edward Allison. All the paintings in the room were forgotten as the four old and new friends conversed. The Allisons had moved to their summer house, Rose explained, so they had not received the letters or calling cards. She and Edward had come to the city just for the day, and once their shopping was completed, had decided to spend an hour at the Academy before returning to their parents' summer place. Would Horace and Elsie come to Elmgrove that very day, both Rose and her brother asked. "Our parents would be so pleased to have you," Rose added, "and my father will be especially glad to meet you, Mr. Dinsmore, for he so values the friendship of your father."

It was agreed. They all went to the hotel first, and Horace treated his guests to a lovely dinner in the dining room, while Aunt Chloe packed several days' clothing for Horace, Elsie, and herself. The carriage ride to the Allisons' was somewhat long, but Elsie, seated beside Rose, found something beautiful or interesting to see along every mile. At last, they came to a driveway arched by elm trees. At its end, Elsie could make out a large, old-fashioned house built of gray stone.

"Is this your house?" Elsie asked. "Oh, it is so pretty."

"I'm glad you think so," Rose said with pleasure. "It is not nearly so grand as Roselands, but my father has made many improvements."

"Just as my Papa did," Elsie said. "You must come and visit The Oaks, Miss Rose. Papa has made such a beautiful home there for us."

"Indeed," Horace added, "Miss Allison and any of her family will always find a warm welcome at The Oaks."

Rose had just time to say, "Thank you," when the carriage stopped near the front steps of Elmgrove. The gentlemen helped Rose and Elsie to the ground, and Rose immediately went to speak to a servant who stood on the piazza. After a few moments, Rose returned to her guests and said, "My mother is napping. She had a bad headache, I'm afraid, so I don't want to disturb her yet. And Father is out on business, but he will be back by supper time. I know they will regret not greeting you both."

"They should have no regrets," Horace replied politely, "for Elsie and I are surprise visitors."

"Then let me show you to your room," Edward Allison said to Horace, "and Rose will serve as Elsie's hostess."

Taking Elsie's hand, Rose led her up the steps and through the door into a large and airy foyer. In the center of the entry room, a broad stairway curled upward in a spiral, and they mounted the steps, Aunt Chloe following close behind. The first room they entered was a high-ceilinged and handsomely furnished bedroom. Through an open door Elsie saw another bedroom, painted in a warm yellow and full of afternoon sunlight.

"This is my room," Rose said to Elsie, "and through there," she pointed to the open door, "is my sister Sophie's room where you will sleep. And I will keep watch over you both."

Elsie darted a quick glance at Aunt Chloe. Sensing Elsie's anxiety, Rose explained, "Aunt Chloe will be staying in her own room in the servants' wing, but she'll attend to you as usual, morning and night. Is that alright with you, Chloe?"

Seeing Aunt Chloe smile with satisfaction, Elsie relaxed. "Oh, I am so glad to be with you again, Miss Rose," she whispered.

"No more than I to have you here, darling," Rose replied, drawing the little girl close and untying the ribbon on Elsie's bonnet. "And are you truly happy now, my dear little friend? I mean, is your life what you hoped it would be?"

"Yes, ma'am," Elsie said fervently. "You've met my Papa, Miss Rose. Do you like him?"

"Very much, so far," Rose said honestly. "It is plain that he is a gracious and handsome gentleman. But more important, I can see that he is a very loving father to you."

"Yes, he is. He loves me every bit as much as I love him," Elsie proclaimed. Then she lowered her head and added, "But he doesn't spoil me, Miss Rose, not at all. I know that I must obey him, promptly and cheerfully. I think I should be an unlucky child if he only indulged and spoiled me."

Rose laughed lightly. "I don't think it would be possible to spoil you, Elsie, darling. But tell me — your Aunt Adelaide wrote to me about your dreadful illness last summer. How I wished I could have comforted you then. Are you feeling quite well now?"

"Almost," Elsie said brightly, "and Papa says this trip should help me get all my strength back. I was very sad last summer, Miss Rose, and very sick, but I always had my Best Friend to comfort me."

"Yes, dear, Jesus is with you always." Rose felt her own throat tighten with emotion. She wrapped her loving arms around Elsie and hugged the child close. "Now, in His goodness, He has brought you here to me."

At just that moment, a flash of blond curls and blue eyes popped around the edge of the hall door and instantly disappeared, moving so quickly that Elsie wondered if she had seen a mirage. But Rose called out, "Sophie! Sophie, come in!" and the curls reappeared atop a little girl of about Elsie's age. Sophie moved cautiously toward her sister and

Elsie; her expression was composed of equal parts of bash-fulness, curiosity, and fun.

"This is Elsie Dinsmore," Rose said, "whom you have so often wished to meet. And Elsie, this is my sister Sophie. Now, girls, I must change for supper, so you two can become acquainted while I dress. Take Elsie into your room, Sophie, and show her where she will sleep. Aunt Chloe will come with you to unpack Elsie's case."

Sophie, her eyes dancing with pleasure, reached for Elsie's hand and said, "I'm ever so glad you are here. Come, and I'll show you my dolls. Rose says that you like dolls, and books, too."

"I do," Elsie responded. "Do you enjoy reading as well? What are your favorite stories?"

And the two little girls fell like lifelong friends into talk and laughter. As they went into the next room, Rose and Aunt Chloe exchanged a few warm words of greeting, for the young lady and Elsie's nursemaid had become close during Rose's visit to Roselands.

"Elsie certainly looks healthy," Rose said, "but has she really recovered?"

"I believe she's almost there, but the doctor wanted her away from the heat back home for the summer," Aunt Chloe explained.

"And her father?" Rose said, not really knowing exactly how to frame her question.

Chloe understood. "Oh, Miss Rose, it's true he nearly killed that child with his hardness, all the time thinking he was doing right. But Jesus saved them both. He lives in Mr. Horace's heart now, and I don't think I've ever seen a finer Christian or a more loving father than that man's become. There's nothing he won't do for his little girl."

Elsie's New Life

"I'm so glad, for Elsie's sake," Rose said. She trusted Chloe's judgment completely, for she had learned at Roselands that Chloe, although a slave and uneducated, was a most observant and intelligent woman and totally devoted to Elsie's welfare.

"I hope their trials are over now," Rose said softly.

"Yes, ma'am, my little Elsie surely does deserve some good times after all she's suffered. And Mr. Horace, too. But you know how troubles are, Miss Rose. They tend to come uninvited and unexpected."

CHAPTER

5

Summer
Friends

*"Perfume and incense bring
joy to the heart, and the
pleasantness of one's
friend springs from
his earnest counsel."*

PROVERBS 27:9

*B*y the time the family gathered in the Elmgrove dining room that evening, Horace and Elsie had met them all, from Mr. Allison and his wife, whose headache, she assured Horace, had been cured by her nap, to baby Daisy, a chipper one-year-old who had already charmed Elsie during a visit to the nursery. The other children were Richard, who was several years younger than Rose; Daniel, a bright boy of thirteen (and not at all like her uncle Arthur, Elsie noticed, though of the same age); seven-year-old Freddie; and little May, a merry four-year-old with the same flaxen curls and sparkling blue eyes as Sophie.

Horace had enjoyed a short talk with Mr. Allison before the supper bell rang and found the older man to be a jovial person and younger-looking than Horace expected the father of so large a brood to be. Mr. Allison was clearly devoted to his Christian faith, his family, and his role as host. Mrs. Allison, though more subdued in her manner than her husband, possessed an equally open and hospitable nature, and her motherly attentions immediately won Elsie's affection.

All the Allisons, save baby Daisy, appeared for the evening meal, and Elsie was seated between her father and Rose.

"Will Elsie have coffee or tea?" Rose asked, addressing her inquiry to Horace.

"Milk if you have it, or water," he replied. "But I seem to remember that Elsie was quite fond of coffee," Rose said, a little surprised.

"Elsie is a very good girl and follows my rules about her diet. I don't allow her coffee nor hot breads such as those," he nodded at a platter piled high with steaming, buttered waffles, "for her health."

"But you will have some waffles, will you not, sir?" asked Mr. Allison.

"I shall, and so will Elsie when she is my age," Horace said, not at all annoyed by the family's questions.

"I think you are quite right, Mr. Dinsmore, to be so careful about Elsie's diet," Mrs. Allison said approvingly. "As I have often said to my husband, I believe we pamper our children's appetites too much. But he is indulgent, and I haven't the firmness to reform our habits by myself."

"You know, my dear," Mr. Allison said bluntly, "that I want my children to be able to enjoy whatever I enjoy."

"On the other hand, children are not adults," Horace said, "and to indulge them now is perhaps to weaken them later on."

Mr. Allison laughed. "You speak as the father of one, and I must admit that I was more strict with Edward and Rose than with my younger children. It happens, you know. A father grows less strict with each new addition and is quite ready to spoil the baby completely. You will see, Horace."

Blushing faintly, Horace replied, "I hope not, Mr. Allison, for if I should ever have more children, I would want to love and guide them equally." With a quick smile at Elsie, Horace then adroitly changed the subject.

Immediately after supper, Mr. Allison called the entire household together for Scripture reading and prayer. Horace expressed his wholehearted approval and told the older man how he had recently instituted the same custom in his own home. The two men and Edward then adjourned to the parlor, and the children scattered to their various interests. Sophie led Elsie outside to play in the garden while it was still light. She showed Elsie to a section of the garden planted with fragrant small bushes and spring flowers.

"These are mine," Sophie said with pride. "I planted them myself, and I tend to them every day."

"Did you dig the earth yourself?" Elsie asked.

"No, Richard and Daniel did that for me. But I water them and pull the weeds and cut the dead blossoms. Maybe you'd like to help me while you're here."

"I would!" Elsie said excitedly. "I've never done gardening before, but we have a very good friend at home — his name is Edward just like your brother — and he has the most beautiful garden and hothouse. If you teach me what to do, maybe I can help him sometime."

"It's hard work, but so much fun to see your own plants grow. Do you think your Papa will allow you to help me, Elsie?" Sophie wondered. "He seems very strict, and not at all like Father."

"Yes," Elsie said slowly, "my Papa is strict, but he's also very kind. He always does what is best for me."

"Let's go inside now," Sophie suggested, for the garden was beginning to fill with the shadows of oncoming night. "I have a beautiful picture book that I know you'll like. But we have to look at it tonight because tomorrow is the Sabbath, and it's not a Sunday book."

The little girls ran inside and entered the parlor where the adults were gathered. The picture book lay open on a corner table, and Elsie and Sophie were soon deeply engaged, looking at and discussing the lovely drawings. Elsie didn't notice the time until Horace spoke to her: "It's eight-thirty, Daughter. Time for you to get to bed."

Elsie's New Life

Elsie rose immediately and went to her father, giving him a kiss on the cheek. "Good night, Papa," she said.

Horace gently stroked her curls and said softly, "God bless and keep you, my little one."

"May I have a kiss, too?" Rose asked, and Elsie skipped over to her friend for another kiss and embrace.

"Now, run along Elsie," Horace instructed. "Go straight to bed after your prayers, and no talking with Miss Sophie."

Sophie, having bid her mother and father good night, joined Elsie, and the two little girls departed for Sophie's room. Chloe was already there, and she helped Elsie to undress and get into her nightclothes. She brushed Elsie's hair, and Sophie's as well, and all the while Sophie was chatting brightly about this and that. But as soon as Elsie retrieved her Bible from her suitcase, Sophie grew still and listened intently as Elsie read a favorite passage. Then both girls prayed silently, and when they had finished, Chloe tucked them in, turned out the lamps, and left.

In the dark, Sophie said in a giggly whisper, "I'm so glad you're here, Elsie. I have ever so much to tell you, and I want to hear all about your home in the South."

"I can't talk now," Elsie said. "Papa told me not to talk at all after I got in bed. I'm sorry, but I can't disobey Papa."

"Oh, pooh!' Sophie said with a little snort. ""He won't care, and besides, he'll never know."

"But God will know," Elsie replied anxiously. "And Papa, too, because I'd have to confess to him that I'd been disobedient. I'd rather be punished than deceive my Papa."

Sophie felt herself flush. "I didn't think about it being deceitful. I'm sorry, Elsie. I would never ask you to do anything wrong. But would your Papa really punish you for such a little thing?"

"Papa says that disobedience is never a little thing, and he always punishes me if I disobey," Elsie explained. "But being punished isn't so bad. The worst is knowing that I would hurt my Papa by disobeying. I love my Papa too much to make him sad."

Sophie made no reply, for she did not want to cause trouble for her new friend. And soon the two girls were sound asleep.

The next day was the Sabbath, and Elsie was up bright and early to join her father for their morning Scripture lesson and prayer. When the bell rang, they joined the Allisons for breakfast and then everyone — excepting the baby, little May, and their nurse — walked to the Allisons' church, which was close by, for morning service. Elsie greatly enjoyed the sermon and was delighted to learn that they would return for the afternoon service. So the whole day was spent in prayer and study of the Holy Word, and after supper that evening, Rose gathered all the children and told them Bible stories. Before bedtime, everyone assembled in the parlor for family worship and hymn-singing, and Elsie went to sleep that night thinking how nice it must be to live at Elmgrove.

Horace had exciting news for her the next morning. "Mr. and Mrs. Allison have invited us to stay here for several weeks," he said. "You and I shall have our morning lessons each day, and Miss Allison has kindly offered to help you with your piano lessons. Then you may do as you like each afternoon, so long as you don't get into any mischief," he added with a wink.

Elsie's New Life

"Oh, Papa," Elsie exclaimed, "this will be so much fun. I was just thinking last night how much I like being here. Everyone is so kind and friendly to us. Do you like the Allisons, Papa?"

"Very much, my dear," he assured her. "It is very pleasant to stop for awhile in so lively a Christian home as this."

"And Miss Rose, Papa. Do you like her?"

"Indeed, Elsie, you are curious this morning. But yes, Miss Allison seems a most gentle and amiable person, and very sweet looking. I look forward to knowing her and all her family better."

Elsie clapped her hands with satisfaction. "I knew you'd like her, Papa," she said happily. "She is the kindest of friends."

And so spring drifted toward summer at Elmgrove. Sophie and Elsie became the fastest of friends, and Sophie grew very fond of Horace, too, when he invited her to join Elsie in their lessons each morning. Rose allowed the two girls to study piano together and taught them several duets, which they played with great enthusiasm. Elsie helped Sophie in the garden each morning for a half hour after breakfast. And with Daniel, the girls were free to play to their hearts' content each afternoon.

Elmgrove was a large property with a stable, barn, and chicken house, wooded areas and a large open field, and an inviting little stream not too far from the house. The children spent long, happy hours running and playing games in the field, searching the woods for wildflowers, hunting for eggs in the barn, building stick houses and playing pretend tea party on the banks of the brook. Sometimes Freddie and May accompanied them, and sometimes two girls who lived nearby came to play after their school day ended. Their names were Hetty and Maggie, and quite nice children they were.

One Friday afternoon at the beginning of June, when Elsie, Sophie, and Daniel were at the brook, making little boats of leaves and twigs, Hetty and Maggie ran into the clearing. Both girls were breathless and beaming.

"We have such exciting news," Hetty burst out.

"A party! Tomorrow!" Maggie proclaimed as she dropped down onto a mossy patch and began to remove her shoes and stockings so she could dangle her feet in the cool stream.

"There's a strawberry field about two miles from here," Hetty said. "Well, about two miles from our schoolhouse, and a group of children are going to walk there tomorrow and spend the day picking berries. We can spend the whole day if we like because it will be Saturday and there's no school."

"Will you come with us?" Maggie asked. "It's going to be such fun!"

"Oh, yes!" Sophie replied excitedly. "I'm sure Mother will allow us to go."

"And you, Elsie? Will you come?" Maggie wanted to know.

"If my Papa agrees," Elsie replied, "and I'm sure he will, for he lets me run and play here all day. Will there be many children?"

Hetty looked at Maggie who said, "I think about a dozen, and there will be several big boys like Daniel. The field belongs to the father of one of our friends, so it will be quite safe."

The children eagerly made their plans for the excursion. Sophie, Daniel, and Elsie would meet the others at the schoolhouse at nine o'clock the next morning, and everyone would bring dinner pails so they could picnic.

When Hetty and Maggie departed, Sophie jumped to her feet. "Let's go ask Mother now," she said, "and your Papa, too, Elsie!"

Returning to the house, they found Mrs. Allison in her sewing room, and though Sophie could barely contain her excitement, she let Daniel do the asking. Elsie, who kept silent throughout, could see that Mrs. Allison was not entirely happy with the plan. The good lady asked many questions and remarked several times that the weather was quite warm and the road would be dusty and the children might easily become overheated and tired.

"If we do, we can come straight home," Daniel said logically. "If anyone becomes too hot or tired, we can easily return at any time."

"Please, Mother," Sophie piped up, for she simply could not keep quiet for long, "Just this once, please let us go."

Reluctantly, Mrs. Allison said, "If you promise to be back here not later than three in the afternoon, and if your father agrees as well, Elsie."

Sophie clapped her hands with glee and threw her arms around Mrs. Allison's neck. "Thank you ever so much, Mother," she exclaimed. Kissing her mother's cheek once more, Sophie jumped up and grabbed Elsie around the waist. "Let's go find your Papa right now," she said, tugging her friend toward the door.

"I'm afraid, girls, that you must wait till supper. Mr. Dinsmore has gone out with Edward for the afternoon," Mrs. Allison said. "Why not go play in Sophie's room and then take a little nap?" she suggested. "You can ask Chloe to wake you when the men return."

The little girls did just that, playing with their dolls for awhile, then settling onto Sophie's wide, soft bed and falling asleep.

It was about an hour later when Elsie felt herself being shaken by a familiar hand.

"You've had a good little nap, darling," Chloe whispered. "If you get up now, we can have you bathed and dressed in time to see your Papa before supper. He and Mr. Edward just rode up."

Elsie sat up immediately, but seeing that Sophie was still sleeping soundly, she carefully got off the bed and tiptoed out of the room with her nursemaid. A short time later, she had been scrubbed clean and dressed in one of her most charming white summer frocks. Chloe quickly brushed Elsie's shining curls, then said, "There now. You look like an angel sure enough. Now run on down to the parlor, 'cause I believe that's where your Papa is, with Mr. Edward and Miss Rose. I'll get Miss Sophie up and ready 'fore the supper bell rings."

Gaily, Elsie danced from the room and headed for the parlor. Seeing her enter, Horace held out his hand to her, and Elsie went to stand at his side. Horace leaned down, kissed her cheek, and placed his arm around her shoulder, but as Edward was talking very earnestly about some scientific matter, Elsie did not interrupt the conversation. From her seat on the couch, Rose observed this little scene with satisfaction; how happy she was to see the affection so plain between her dear little friend and Horace.

At last — for what were merely minutes but seemed endless to Elsie — Edward excused himself, and Horace turned his full attention on his daughter. "Did you enjoy yourself today?" he asked.

Elsie's New Life

"Yes, Papa. And I have something to ask you. Please, say yes, Papa. Please, do!" she said excitedly.

"Why, Elsie," Horace said with a smile, "you know I cannot say yes before I have heard your request. Now, tell me what it is you want."

Quickly Elsie explained about the strawberry field and the children's party and the invitation from Maggie and Hetty. She gave him all the details of the plan and came to an end with a pleading little voice: "Mrs. Allison says we may go if you agree, Papa. Please say yes, Papa. Sophie and Daniel will be so disappointed if we can't go, and it will be so much fun. Oh, Papa, won't you let me go? *Please*!"

When she finished, Elsie hardly dared to draw a breath. She tried to read her father's expression, but could see only that he was in deep thought. At length he spoke, gently but firmly: "No, dearest, I cannot allow you to go. I don't approve of this plan at all."

Tears sprang to her eyes, and Elsie opened her mouth to protest. She said nothing, however, because she knew how her father hated coaxing and begging. But she could not control her tears.

In a low and serious tone, Horace said, "Tears will not do, Elsie. Go up to my room now, and stay there until you can wear a pleasant face again. You may come down when you judge yourself to be ready for the company of others."

Elsie bit her lip and hurried from the parlor, running headlong into Richard in the hall. He reached out and steadied her before she could fall.

"Tears!" he exclaimed, seeing her wet face and fearing that she was hurt. "Are you alright?"

"Yes," Elsie gulped. She pulled away and said as she ran across the hallway, "I must go now."

Richard could only watch as she disappeared up the stairs. But her tears disturbed him, for like all the Allisons, he had become very fond of this new, little friend from the South. A moment later, Rose came out the parlor door and to his side.

"What is wrong with our guest?" Richard asked with the concern clear in his voice.

"I'm not sure," Rose said softly. "She seemed to be asking her father for something, and then suddenly she rushed from the room. I fear he has sent her upstairs as a punishment."

"Whatever for?" Richard demanded. "She's such a dear little girl. I can't believe she deserved his anger, although he seems excessively strict with her."

"I didn't say he was angry," Rose corrected. "And since we do not know what happened, we shouldn't make judgments too quickly."

"You're right, of course," Richard said, a little abashed by his own hastiness. "Still, I am sorry to see her so sad."

Upstairs, Elsie shut herself inside her father's room and had a good cry. But presently, the tears ceased, and she found a handkerchief to wipe her face. "What a silly way to behave," she thought to herself, "crying just because I didn't get my way. I know that Papa has a good reason for saying no, but I didn't give him a chance to tell me why. I just cried from disappointment, like a baby. And I made a scene in front of Miss Allison and Richard, too. What must they think of me?"

Elsie went to her father's mirror and looked at her tear-streaked face. "Well, I can be pleasant, just as Papa said, because he wouldn't do anything he didn't think was best for me." As she patted at her curls and dabbed the handkerchief at her eyes, she suddenly remembered an incident that happened when Horace had first come to Roselands. He had forbidden her to play in the meadow, and she had disobeyed. She had thought his punishment so unfair, until she learned the reason. There were rattlesnakes in the meadow at Roselands that spring, and Horace's strict rule was to protect her from danger.

"Elsie Dinsmore," she said aloud to her reflection, "you must trust Papa always, and not think that you know best. Now, be cheerful, and you can go downstairs and show Papa how much you love and respect him."

Straightening her little shoulders and smoothing her dress, she smiled at her reflection and then marched from the room just as the supper bell rang. Taking her place beside Horace at the dinner table, she looked up into his face. His warm smile told her what she needed to know — that all was forgiven — and she felt so relieved that she beamed with happiness.

Seeing Elsie's and Horace's happy expressions across the table, Sophie and Daniel naturally assumed that Horace had given his permission for the strawberry party — doubling their disappointment when, in the garden after supper, Elsie informed them of her Papa's actual decision.

Sophie pouted, and Daniel frowned deeply. "But why?" he asked, and Elsie was at a loss, because she could not explain her father's thinking.

"Why all the long faces?" asked Richard, who had come outside to join the younger children for a game. When they explained, Richard turned to Elsie and said, "So that's why you were crying this afternoon."

Seeing Elsie's deep blush, Richard added quickly, "Never mind it. Why, we've all shed tears over things a lot less important than a party. Say, I came out to play a game. How about tag? Trees are safe, and I'll be 'it'!"

In a few minutes, they were all running around the garden, laughing gaily and forgetting all about their thwarted plans. Freddie and even little May soon joined their romps. After some time, however, Elsie grew tired, and seeing her father sitting alone on the piazza, she left the group and went to him.

Hanging her head, she said, "I'm sorry, Papa, for the way I behaved this afternoon. I know that you always do what is right for me, but I forgot."

Horace gently lifted her chin. "I would like you to trust my decisions whether or not you understand my reasons. Elsie, you must believe that I do not make decisions lightly or without sufficient reason, even if I cannot always explain them to you."

"I do believe that, Papa," Elsie said earnestly.

"I think that you do," Horace replied with a smile. Then he went on, "I know that you are unhappy about missing the party, but you are not yet as strong as you should be. You are not yet ready for a long walk in the hot sun and hours of picking berries in the field. There is every possibility that you might become ill, and I will take no chance with your health. Understand, dear Daughter, that I am well aware of your disappointment, and I take no pleasure in thwarting your desire."

"I know, Papa," Elsie said softly, "And I'm very sorry I let my feelings show without thinking."

Horace tousled her curls and spoke heartily, "Well, perhaps we can make up for your loss. I have been talking with

Elsie's New Life

Mr. and Mrs. Allison, and I believe we have an even better idea for tomorrow."

Elsie's bright eyes rounded with excitement. "What, Papa?" she asked.

"Oh, I think it will be even more fun if it is a surprise," Horace said, adopting a mysterious tone. "You tell the other children to be ready for a ride after breakfast in the morning. Wear play clothes and be on the piazza at a quarter to nine."

"But where are we going, Papa?"

"Ah, dearest, telling would ruin the surprise. Be patient, and you will be rewarded."

No one — not even Richard — knew what the adults had in store, and Sophie was particularly hard pressed to keep from talking after she and Elsie went to bed that night. But morning came, as it always does, and the girls — dressed in their light muslin frocks and pinafores — were at the breakfast table before anyone else, hoping for some clue about the surprise. The adults arrived, however, wearing straight faces and refusing to answer any questions. Mr. Allison and Horace talked about business; Mrs. Allison, Rose, and Edward chatted about some friends who were traveling to Europe that summer. The children were so excited and curious that they could hardly eat, but at last the meal was done, and after the family devotion, Mr. Allison made much ado about looking at his heavy pocket watch.

With mock seriousness, he said, "I see that it is now half past eight. I believe there is time for the girls to get their bonnets, isn't there, Mother?"

Smiling broadly, Mrs. Allison nodded. "Sophie and Elsie," she said, "will see that May has her cap, too, won't you, girls? Daniel, take Freddie to wash his hands and face, for he seems to have gotten more jam on his outside than his inside this morning. You have fifteen minutes, children. Now run along, and we will see you shortly."

The children ran to complete their various chores, and at the end of the allotted time, they all assembled with their parents on the piazza. In the driveway, they saw not only the family carriage but three saddled horses and a large, horse-drawn farm wagon, its floor covered in fresh straw.

"I believe the time has arrived to reveal the surprise," Mr. Allison said to Horace.

"Indeed, sir," Horace replied, smiling, "or else these children may explode with curiosity."

Looking over the little crowd of upturned faces, Mr. Allison began, "It seems you were looking forward to a day of strawberrying. Well, although one plan has failed, another has come along. We shall all enjoy a party. Edward knows a nearby farm where we can purchase not only strawberries but fresh cream as well. We will enjoy a nice ride and a picnic and end our party with strawberries and cream. Is that a plan that pleases?"

Elsie and Sophie both clapped their hands with joy. Little May danced on her toes, and Daniel said brightly, "Oh, bravo, Father!" Freddie could hardly contain himself. "Yippee!" he crowed.

"Then let's be on our way," Mr. Allison said. "Your mother, Rose, and May will ride in the carriage with the picnic baskets. Mr. Dinsmore and Edward and I will take the horses. And the rest of you shall have a hayride in the wagon. Now everybody get to your places!"

"Wait, Father," Sophie said anxiously, tugging at his coat.

"What is it, dear? Why has your face clouded up so?"

Elsie's New Life

"It's the other children, Father. Maggie and Hetty and all their friends. I just remembered that they will be waiting for us at the schoolhouse. What will they think if we don't come?"

Mr. Allison scooped up his daughter, and as he carried her toward the wagon, he announced to one and all, "We haven't forgotten your friends. Mr. Dinsmore's servant, John, went to Maggie's home last night to deliver a message to her parents."

"Yes," said Horace as he hoisted Elsie onto the soft straw in the wagon, "and I believe there are quite a few children waiting for us at the schoolhouse right now."

Elsie's eyes glowed with delight. "Are they coming with us, Papa?"

"Yes, dear. The invitation was issued and accepted last night."

Mr. Allison laughed. "Why, we must have more children to fill this cart and to eat all the picnic food. Mrs. Allison has prepared enough good things for an army," he said happily. "I believe this will be a Saturday we shall not soon forget!"

How right he was. The strawberry party was a grand success, and many happy little heads lay on their pillows that night, remembering a day filled with games and stories, delicious food and the fun of riding in the big hay wagon. And all the children had taken home a basket brimming with ripe strawberries for their families, for as Rose told them, the best part of having fun is sharing it with others.

CHAPTER

An Adventure
Continued

"Many are the plans in a man's heart, but it is the Lord's purpose that prevails."

PROVERBS 19:21

*S*ummer came to Elmgrove, and Elsie bloomed as bright and healthy as the Allisons' gardens. The country air, the pleasant climate, the company of so many good friends, and the loving attention of her father — all the elements conspired to return her to the good health she had enjoyed before her terrible illness.

"Why, your daughter seems to be growing taller and stronger every day," Mrs. Allison declared one morning as she and Rose chatted with Horace on the piazza.

"Yes," Horace said with a smile. "Thanks to your generous display of hospitality to unexpected guests, I believe Elsie has recovered all her old energy and good cheer."

He looked toward the garden where Elsie and Sophie were busily weeding and watering Sophie's little patch of flowers. Every now and then, the girls' laughter would ring out across the lawn.

"Why, Horace, you and your daughter are more like family than guests in our home," Mrs. Allison protested. "Elsie is such a wonderful playmate for Sophie and the other children. And you, sir — well, just the other night, Mr. Allison was saying how pleasant it is to have a young man of your knowledge and experience to talk with. And I have noticed how Edward seems to thrive in the company of one who shares his interests in science and politics."

"We live in an exciting age," Horace replied, "and Edward is a remarkably bright and capable young man. He reminds me, in fact, of a dear friend — another Edward, by the way — with whom I have spent countless hours discussing every subject under the sun."

Elsie's New Life

"That would be Edward Travilla?" Rose asked. "I met his mother once, just before I left Roselands."

"He is my truest friend," Horace said, remembering how Edward Travilla had tried to sway him from his near-disastrous course with Elsie and supported him throughout those terrible weeks and months when Elsie's life hung in the balance. "Like your Edward, my old friend is both forthright and gifted with intelligence. And he rarely hesitates to tell me when I am wrong," Horace added with a laugh.

"Do you miss your home and friends in the South?" Mrs. Allison inquired. "You've been away for several months now."

"One always misses home, I suppose," Horace said, "but travel is a great pleasure for me, and Elsie seems to have inherited my curiosity about people and places."

"She was describing Washington to Sophie and me just the other night," Rose said, "and she certainly seems to have learned a great deal during your stop there. Her recounting of the story of Mrs. Madison and George Washington's portrait was particularly spirited."

"It's good, I think, for children to know all we can teach them of history," Horace commented. "It prepares them to become good citizens. And you, Miss Rose, do you enjoy travel?"

"I do, sir," Rose responded, her face brightening at the subject. "It is hard for Mother and Father to take so large a family on long trips, but we have been to Washington and New York, and I greatly enjoyed my visit to the South. Someday, I hope to see Europe."

"You would enjoy it immensely," Horace said warmly. "With your love of music and art, you would appreciate the culture there. The museums and galleries, the symphonies, the architecture—"

Mrs. Allison laughed, "I would enjoy seeing those sights myself, Horace, but I'm afraid by the time Daisy and May are old enough for that kind of trip, I shall be quite too old and worn-out for the journey."

"One is never too old for travel," Horace replied, "and I cannot imagine you or Mr. Allison will ever lack the energy to do what you want."

"Well, Paris will have to wait for me," Mrs. Allison said gaily as she rose from her seat. "I have a nursery of little ones to tend to at the moment."

She excused herself, and after a few minutes more of chatting, Rose and Horace also went to their morning duties. But the conversation had planted the seed of an idea in Horace's thoughts, and that evening he approached Mr. Allison with a proposal.

Several evenings later, Horace asked Elsie to join him for a short walk after supper. As they strolled down a path lined with rose bushes and fragrant jasmine, he asked, "Have you enjoyed our stay with the Allisons, dear Daughter?"

"Oh, yes, Papa," Elsie answered enthusiastically. "Mr. and Mrs. Allison are so kind, and I almost think of Sophie and the others as my own brothers and sisters. And being with Miss Rose — Papa, she really loves me, you know. She is so sweet and good to me."

"I'm glad you like it here," Horace said, "and Elmgrove certainly agrees with you. But, dearest, we are only guests and must not overstay our welcome."

Elsie's New Life

Elsie's grip on her father's hand tightened. She knew at once what he was about to say.

"I'm afraid we must be leaving very soon," Horace continued, his voice deep and solemn. "We are expected in New York in another week, and we have reservations in Boston for a week after that."

Working very hard to control her feeling of disappointment, Elsie said softly, "Those will be very interesting places, Papa, and they are on my list. I will only be a little sad to leave here."

If Elsie had looked up, she might have seen the smile on her father's face. "Poor child, I know this is bad news to you," he said, keeping his voice serious. "But perhaps I can give you some news that is good."

At this Elsie did look up, and her father's happy expression surprised her. She was even more astonished when he asked, "What would you say if Miss Rose and Mr. Edward accompanied us on our trip?"

Elsie could manage only a questioning "Sir?" in response.

"It's true, Elsie. Mr. and Mrs. Allison have agreed to allow Mr. Edward and Miss Rose to join our party. After New York and Boston, we will tour New England and visit Niagara Falls. And I have arranged for us to stay for several weeks at a lovely hotel and spa at the end of our trip, before the Allisons return to Philadelphia and we to The Oaks. Do you think this is a good plan?"

"It's wonderful, Papa!" Elsie exclaimed. "Miss Rose will be going with us," she chirped. "Dear, dear Miss Rose!"

"And Mr. Edward," Horace added.

"Yes, Papa, Mr. Edward, too. I like him very much. But I love Miss Rose the best of all. Don't you, Papa?"

An Adventure Continued

Horace was only a little disconcerted by Elsie's question. "I think Miss Rose is very lovely," he said in a neutral tone, "and I know how much she cares for you. That makes me happy."

~~~~~~~

The departure from Elmgrove was bittersweet. Elsie was anxious to continue her journey now that Rose Allison would be among her companions; all the same, she was sad to be leaving her new, good friends, and it was especially hard to part from Sophie.

"Please, can't Elsie stay with us?" Sophie pleaded to Horace on the night before the leave-taking. "She can live with us and be my sister."

"But then I would be dreadfully lonely without her," Horace replied gently. "She is my only child, and if you keep her, I will have no one to share my life and home."

Sophie bowed her blond head and said, "I didn't think of that, Mr. Dinsmore. I don't want you to be lonely."

Horace took Sophie's little chin in his hand and raised her face. He saw two tears trembling on her eyelashes. In his kindest way, he said, "But you must make me a promise, Miss Sophie. You must promise to come and visit us at The Oaks any time you wish. I have enjoyed our lessons together very much, and I would like to be your host in my home. You'll always be welcome there — you and your family."

Sophie's expression brightened. "Really, Mr. Dinsmore?" she asked. "May I really visit you?"

"As Elsie must have told you, I am a man of my word," Horace answered with a warm smile. "And I give you my word that The Oaks will always be open to you and your family."

Sophie was as satisfied as she could be, but still it was hard to say good-bye the next morning, and the travelers departed in a mixture of laughter and tears. As the carriage followed the road back to Philadelphia, where their train to New York awaited, Elsie leaned her head against Rose's shoulder and said, "You are so fortunate, Miss Rose."

"Why, dearest?" the young woman asked.

"To have so many brothers and sisters who love you."

"But you have many people who love you," Rose said reassuringly.

"And nobody better than my Papa," Elsie said. "But brothers and sisters are different, Miss Rose. They're like special friends."

With a little smile at Edward, who was listening to this conversation, Rose replied, "Yes, they are, dear. Very special friends."

CHAPTER

An Unexpected
Problem

*"Love is patient,
love is kind."*

1 CORINTHIANS 13:4

An Unexpected Problem

The sitting room of Horace and Elsie's large, second-story suite opened onto a balcony. From this porch, the view was truly spectacular, like a landscape painting. In the foreground the hotel's green lawn rolled downward toward a sward of trees dressed in the deep green shades of late summer. Beyond the trees, the land seemed to rise again, fading into a broad stretch of glittering water that took its color from the clear, blue sky and its sparkle from the sun. Beyond the water, which was one of New England's most famous rivers, the land rose up again in high, ragged, stone cliffs. Lush forests added more shades of green, and behind the trees, mist-shrouded peaks jutted toward the sky.

Elsie leaned against the railing of the porch and said, "I think I will like it here, Papa."

Horace, who sat in a wicker chair nearby, reading his newspaper, replied, "I'm glad, dearest. I have stayed here before, and I hoped it would please you and the Allisons. I wanted us to end our vacation in a most enjoyable fashion. I think you'll find much to occupy your time, and the guests are generally quite nice people. In fact, I believe I saw some children of your age in the drawing room last night when we arrived."

"May we take a walk now, Papa? I see paths into the woods over there."

"We can, dear, as soon as Miss Rose and Edward are ready to join us."

"Then may I go to their rooms, Papa?"

"You may."

Elsie's New Life

Elsie skipped away, intending to go straight to the Allisons' suite on the opposite side of the large building. But before Horace could read one more paragraph of his newspaper article, she was back at his side.

"Papa," she whined. "It's something bad."

Dropping his paper to his lap, Horace looked into his daughter's face.

"What is so bad?" he asked. "I've rarely seen you looking this displeased."

"I went into the hallway, and guess who I saw. Guess who I saw coming out of the room across the hall."

"Miss Stevens?"

Elsie was astonished. "How did you know, Papa?"

Horace smiled. "I didn't read your mind, dear. I saw her name on the hotel book when I registered ours last night."

"But doesn't this just spoil everything, Papa? Miss Stevens will want to be with you and me all the time, and you know how I feel about her."

"I do, Elsie, but I expect she will be less troublesome than you expect. If you stick close by my side, I doubt she will annoy you. Just be polite, and stay close to me or Miss Rose and Edward. That should take care of the situation."

Elsie laughed. "Then I'll stick to you like a honeysuckle vine."

Horace was rising, for he had heard a knock at the door of the suite. "I expect that's the Allisons," he said. "You run get your bonnet from Aunt Chloe, and we'll be ready for that walk."

An Unexpected Problem

Unfortunately, Horace's prediction was not as accurate as Elsie hoped. It was Miss Stevens who proved to be the honeysuckle vine, following Elsie's trail and winding round the little girl at every opportunity. In the days that followed, whatever Elsie tried to do on her own — walking in the garden, reading a book on the hotel veranda, writing letters in the lounge — Miss Stevens always found her.

The lady had not changed much since Elsie last saw her. She was still very pretty and always dressed in the height of fashion. And she still petted and flattered Elsie mercilessly. How good it was to see Elsie and her father again! How sweet and pretty Elsie was! How kind Mr. Dinsmore was, and so handsome! How everyone admired his fine manners and entertaining conversation!

Miss Stevens tried to ingratiate herself with father and daughter in every imaginable way. To Horace's face, she praised his parenting abilities, telling him that only a wise father could raise so lovely and obedient a daughter. Behind his back, she tempted Elsie with sweets and presents and promises.

One morning, when Elsie thought she had secured some privacy in the empty hotel parlor, Miss Stevens appeared.

"How charming you look today," the lady gushed. "But Elsie dear, I would love to see you in dresses that aren't so plain. Why, the fashion is for flounces on young girls' skirts, and you would look so beautiful in a dress with lots of ruffles and ribbons."

Before Elsie could get out a word of protest, Miss Stevens went gabbling on, "I know! I shall have a new dress made for you. I'm sure your father won't object to a little gift like that. He's so proud of you. But gentlemen are the last to think of things like fashion, my dear. That is a mother's duty, don't you think? Oh, Elsie, you should have a mother to dress you prettily — you dear, little thing."

Struggling not to let her irritation show, Elsie replied, "Thank you, Miss Stevens. Your offer is most kind. But I do not need a mother or a new dress. Papa buys all my dresses himself, and I like the ones he chooses. He says little girls shouldn't be loaded with flounces and finery, and I think he's right. He says my clothes should be neat and simple in style, but made of the finest materials and by the best dressmakers. And I agree."

"Oh, so do I," Miss Stevens asserted, trying to hide her mistake. "I can see that your dresses are not cheap and are certainly well made. It's only that I think you would be so very pretty with a little more ornament. More pretty ruffles, and more jewelry. You wear very little jewelry, Elsie dear. Perhaps some gold bracelets like mine. See how pretty they are?"

Miss Stevens was leaning close over Elsie's shoulder now, and the little girl felt desperate to escape.

"Thank you. Miss Stevens, but I only wear what my Papa chooses for me," she said quickly. "Excuse me! There's Miss Rose, and I must go!"

Dashing away from the overbearing woman, Elsie ran to the veranda, where she had heard Rose's welcome voice.

"Elsie dear," Rose said. "I was looking for you. Your Papa and Edward are just coming, and we're all going for a walk."

With more gratitude than this simple announcement deserved, Elsie said, "Thank you, Miss Rose. Thank you *so* very much. I'll just go get my bonnet."

As Elsie disappeared, Miss Stevens came through the parlor door and approached Rose.

"I think I heard that you are going for a walk," Miss Stevens said, "and I hope you will let me invite myself to

accompany you. I have been waiting for some pleasant company. Just let me get my hat, and I will be right back."

Rose found herself unable to respond before Miss Stevens was gone through the door again. But she was able to tell Horace and Edward what had transpired when they arrived.

Horace said nothing, but his dark look betrayed his annoyance. Like Elsie, he was growing quite tired of being polite to Miss Stevens.

"I think Miss Stevens should take her walks at the bottom of the sea," Edward commented with disgust.

Rose laughed. "No, you don't, Edward. You know you would be the first to jump to her rescue if she fell into the sea."

A grumbled "Humph!" was all Edward could reply before Miss Stevens, and Elsie behind her, reappeared. Before anything could be said, the lady moved to Horace's side and took his arm firmly.

"I never stand on ceremony with old friends, Mr. Dinsmore," she said archly. "It has never been my way."

Horace, turning quickly to offer his other arm to Rose, said flatly, "I agree, Miss Stevens. It has never been your way."

Rose was inclined to reject Horace's courtesy, because the graveled path was really too narrow for three people to walk abreast. But the pleading look in Horace's eyes instantly changed her mind, and she took his arm. Edward and Elsie were left to bring up the rear, and though Edward tried to be a gracious escort, both he and Elsie were too provoked to be good company. All-in-all, the excursion was most uncomfortable for everyone except Miss Stevens. She talked and laughed incessantly, addressing her conversation solely to Horace, and receiving his polite responses as if they were the most brilliant comments.

In truth, what most angered Horace was Miss Stevens's continual rudeness to Rose. The snobbish woman habitually interrupted any conversation he undertook with Rose, and she addressed Rose in a snide and sneering manner that was obvious to everyone. It cost Horace tremendous effort to maintain a respectful politeness to this irritating and self-centered young woman.

So Horace was inwardly sympathetic when, returning to their rooms after their unpleasant walk, Elsie exploded, "She's just too awful, Papa! She spoiled our walk entirely!"

"Who is 'she'?" Horace asked calmly.

"Miss Stevens, of course!" Elsie exclaimed.

"Then use her name, dear. It is disrespectful for a child your age to address a lady as 'you' or 'she.' She is *Miss* Stevens, just as Edward Allison is Mr. Allison or Mr. Edward. They are your elders, Elsie, and always deserve the courtesy of their titles."

"I know, Papa," Elsie said. "But Miss Stevens is so impolite."

"That makes no difference," Horace said seriously. "Although Miss Stevens is the last person on whom you should model your behavior. The less you resemble her in manners or dress or anything else, the better. If you want to copy anyone, let it be Miss Rose, for she is a perfect lady in every respect."

"Miss Rose is kind to everyone, Papa," Elsie said. "Have you heard how Miss Stevens treats the servants? She's always so cross with them, and she orders them around in such a hateful manner."

"Elsie!" Horace snapped.

Surprised by his tone, she instantly came to attention.

In a softer voice, Horace said, "Come here and sit beside me, dear. I need to talk with you."

When Elsie had taken her place next to her father on the couch, he continued, "I've noticed lately that you are becoming most critical of others. Have you forgotten that we do not judge other people's faults?"

"I'm sorry, Papa," Elsie said with genuine contrition. "It's no excuse, but Miss Stevens is always after me about something or other, and I wish I could tell her just to leave me alone."

"I understand," Horace said kindly, "but you cannot do that. You must always behave with courtesy to Miss Stevens, even though she does not. God sends us little trials as well as the great ones, Elsie, so we can learn to bear them with patience. Do you remember these verses from the first chapter of the Book of James?" he asked, and then he quoted: "'Consider it pure joy, my brothers, whenever you face trials of many kinds, because you know that the testing of your faith develops perseverance. Perseverance must finish its work so that you may be mature and complete, not lacking anything.' These trifling vexations — for Miss Stevens's behavior is only a small annoyance — are tests of our spirit of forgiveness. The Bible teaches us to be courteous and to treat others as we wish to be treated."

"You're always courteous, Papa," Elsie commented. "I was wondering how you could be so nice when Miss Stevens interrupted our walk and then took your arm without being asked."

Horace laughed. "I doubt you would have objected if Miss Rose had done the same thing," he said.

"Miss Rose would *never* do such a thing," Elsie said firmly.

"No, she wouldn't," Horace agreed. "I admit to you, Daughter, that I don't find Miss Stevens to be very agreeable company, but I have an obligation to her, and so do you."

Elsie looked doubtful, so Horace continued, "Miss Stevens is the daughter of a fine gentlemen who once saved your grandfather's life. Because I owe her father such a debt of gratitude, I must always show my respect to his daughter."

Interested now, Elsie asked her father for the story.

"Well," Horace began, "it happened when your grandfather and Mr. Stevens were very young, before either was married. It was an unusually cold winter in the South, and some of the ponds had frozen over. The two young men were out in the fields one day, and your grandfather tried walking on a frozen pond. But the ice was thin, and it broke under his weight. Your grandfather fell into the cold water and would have drowned that day, had not Mr. Stevens risked his own life to save him. So you see, without Mr. Stevens, neither you nor I would be here today."

Elsie's hazel eyes were round with wonder, for she could almost see the scene as her father described it. Mr. Stevens must have been a very brave man, she thought.

"I believe we can spare some extra courtesies for Miss Stevens, don't you?" Horace asked, smiling broadly as Elsie nodded her assent.

Elsie's patience was tested to the limit several days later. For once, Miss Stevens was nowhere to be seen, and Elsie was having great fun playing paper dolls with several other girls on the veranda.

They were all chatting about this and that when one of the girls asked, "Will you like your new mother, Elsie?"

Stunned by the question, Elsie dropped her scissors and turned to the little girl. "New mother?" she exclaimed. "What are you talking about, Annie? I'm not going to have any new mother."

But little Annie was quite sure of her facts. "Yes you are," she insisted. "I heard my Mamma tell my Papa about it. My Mamma said that Miss Stevens told her so herself."

"And what does Miss Stevens know about anything?" Elsie demanded indignantly.

"She ought to know," the other girl laughed, "since she is the one who is going to marry your father."

"She isn't! That's false! She —" Elsie suddenly remembered her father's admonition and clamped her mouth shut. "Have patience and persevere," she thought to herself.

"But it's true, and everybody in the hotel is talking about it," Annie said heatedly, for she did not like being accused of a falsehood. "My Mamma wondered if you knew and how you would like having Miss Stevens as your mother. And my Papa said he wondered if your Papa knew how much Miss Stevens flirted at the parties here before you ever came to the hotel."

Elsie could take no more. She jumped to her feet, scattering bits of paper everywhere, and ran from the veranda, through the lobby, up the stairs, and into the suite. Breathlessly, she cried out to her father, "Oh, Papa. It's — it's that hateful Miss Stevens!"

Then she burst into tears and collapsed on Horace's chest. For once, he let her cry, stroking her hair until the storm had passed. When she had calmed, he wiped her eyes with his handkerchief and gently asked for an explanation.

"Miss Stevens has told everyone that she will be my new mother," Elsie managed to say between gasps. "She is such a hateful, hateful person, Papa."

Horace laid his finger on her lips. "Don't use that word again, Elsie," he said. "It is not the kind of language I expect from you."

"I'm sorry," Elsie responded, dropping her head. "But they are all talking about you, Papa, and it's so unfair. I even heard John and Pearl, Miss Stevens's maid, talking last night, and Pearl said that she would get you to marry her — "

"Marry Pearl?" Horace broke in with a laugh.

"No, Papa. Miss Stevens, of course. Please don't tease me."

Horace lifted Elsie from his chest and set her next to him.

"You know better than to listen to idle gossip, Elsie," he said. "Remember the last time?" Elsie nodded, and Horace went on, "You must remember what I told you then. I would never marry anyone who does not meet your complete approval. Now, tell me what you have heard, and we'll see if we can set the record straight."

As Elsie revealed all that little Annie had said, Horace's expression became increasingly serious. When she finished, he said, "Poor child, I am sorry you have been subjected to this kind of talk. I know that we should ignore such troublesome gossips, but sometimes it is wiser to get away from them. Would you like to go home, dearest?"

Elsie's first reaction was an instantaneous "Yes!" The idea of escaping from Miss Stevens and returning to the security of The Oaks was powerful. But a moment later, she remembered their companions: "But we can't leave Miss Rose and Mr. Edward, can we?"

"They will understand, dear, for the situation has been almost as difficult for them as for you and me."

"Maybe we could invite Miss Rose to come home with us," Elsie suggested hopefully. "She could stay the whole winter, just as she did at Roselands."

Horace flushed slightly as he said, "No, Elsie dear, that is not possible."

"Why not, Papa?" she wondered.

"Because it would be improper for me to invite an unmarried lady into my home," he explained quickly. Then Elsie slumped against him with a sigh, and for several minutes the two sat in silence.

At length, Horace spoke up. "Elsie, would you like very much for Miss Rose to come to The Oaks and live with us?"

Elsie straightened and looked into her father's eyes. All of a sudden, she understood exactly what her father was asking. "Yes, sir," she replied with feeling. "*Very* much."

"I will do nothing unless it pleases you, dear. I once made a vow to do everything in my power to make your life happy, and I would not take a step as important as this if I thought it would hurt you."

He put a gentle arm around her and hugged her close.

Softly, Elsie asked the questions that were uppermost in her thoughts: "Will it make you happy, Papa? And do you think my Mamma will be happy?"

"I believe your mother loves us both too well not to be pleased with anything that increases our happiness," he said.

"And do you love Miss Rose better than Mamma," she asked, almost afraid of his reply.

Elsie's New Life

Horace did not hesitate. "I do not love her more or less, Elsie dearest. Your mother will always be in my heart, as you are always in my heart. But there is room there for Rose as well. You see, darling, I have learned from our Lord and Savior that the heart is an endless well of love. I can open my heart to Rose, and it will not change my feelings for your mother or you or anyone else I love. Yes, I do love Rose, very, very much."

"I have one more question, Papa, if you will not be angry with me."

"No, darling. Ask all the questions you like."

"Do you think my Mamma will be unhappy if I call Miss Rose 'Mamma'?"

"I think your mother would like it very much," Horace said softly, recalling the lovely face of the young woman who had been his first love. "Your mother was a generous and caring person who wanted only the best for you. I think she would be most pleased if you share the name 'Mamma' with Rose."

Elsie thought for a few moments. "I'm sure that you're right, Papa," she said finally. "My Mamma would love Rose as you and I do. And I will be very happy to be her daughter. But Papa —" she hesitated until a small smile stole across her father's face. "Papa, I think I can never love anyone so well as I love you."

Horace encircled her in his arms and kissed her cheeks. "That is more than I have a right to expect," he said almost in a whisper.

Father and daughter sat silently for several minutes more, each contemplating the momentous step they were about to take. Then Elsie suddenly had another question.

"Papa, have you asked Miss Rose yet?"

An Unexpected Problem

Horace suddenly roared with laughter. "No, dear," he managed to say. "Poor Rose knows nothing of our plans. Perhaps she will not agree to take on the two of us. I've heard it said that ladies do not want to marry a man with children."

"That's silly, Papa," Elsie replied with a little pout. "Miss Stevens certainly doesn't care that you have a daughter."

Horace laughed again. "But Miss Stevens is certainly no Rose Allison."

"I know, Papa, and that is why Miss Rose will truly love us both," Elsie said with great earnestness. "You must ask her soon, Papa. We can't go home until she has agreed to come and be my Mamma!"

"I promise, Elsie, that I will ask her at the earliest possible moment."

That night after supper, a large group gathered for an evening horseback ride. Miss Stevens was in the party, as well as Edward Allison. But much to Miss Steven's consternation (and Edward's satisfaction, for he had guessed what was afoot), neither Horace Dinsmore nor Rose Allison had appeared when the party set out from the hotel.

Upstairs in her room, Elsie read for awhile. Then she approached Chloe, who was laying out her little charge's clothes for the next day, and made an old, familiar request.

"Tell me about my Mamma, please, Aunt Chloe," she asked. Although she had heard the stories hundreds of times before, on this night of all nights, Elsie felt the need to be close to her precious, unknown mother whose image had been enshrined in her heart for as long as she could remember.

8

Telling Hard Truths

*"Create in me a pure heart,
O God, and renew a
steadfast spirit
within me."*

PSALMS 51:10

*H*orace had taken Rose aside at supper and asked her to forgo the horseback ride that evening. He hoped, he said, that she would join him for a walk instead. Rose readily agreed, and a while later they were strolling one of the hotel's charming wooded pathways.

Normally, Horace was the most interesting of companions, but Rose was unable to engage him on any subject this night. She tried one topic after another, but in response, she received only the most perfunctory of answers. When she proposed that Elsie might join them on their walk — the little girl could always cheer her father — Horace replied that Elsie had taken enough exercise for the day. Rose was at a loss to explain Horace's strange mood; he was not angry, she could tell, nor depressed. So she too fell silent.

At length, they came to a rustic bench in a small clearing, and Horace bade Rose to sit and rest for awhile. The moon had risen and it bathed the little stopping place in a circle of soft, white light. The air was pleasantly warm, and a gentle breeze touched their faces. For some time, the only sounds that broke the silence were the soft rustling of the trees and the distant song of a night bird.

Rose was beginning to become uncomfortable, for she had no idea what was causing Horace's behavior. Then Horace spoke up, his voice deep and mellow.

"Miss Allison," he said, "I have a story to tell you, if you will oblige me."

"Of course, Mr. Dinsmore," she replied in relief. "I always find your stories interesting."

Elsie's New Life

"This is not like my usual stories," he said, and Rose thought she heard a little quiver in his tone. "But it is one that must be told. It began about a dozen years ago with a wild and reckless young man of seventeen. This boy had been much spoiled by the indulgences of his doting father, who loved him as the only child of his beloved, dead wife. It was summer, and the young man was spending several months with friends in one of our large cities to the south, a long way from his father's home. There he met and fell desperately in love with a beautiful girl — an orphan and heiress some two years younger than he.

"The young man knew that his father and her guardian would never approve of a marriage between young people of such tender years. He also knew that his father, a man of immense family pride, would object to the union as socially unsuitable. You see, the girl's father, although he had achieved wealth and position through his own labor and dedication, had begun life poor and uneducated."

Here Horace paused for a moment, and Rose, understanding just who the 'wild and reckless young man' of the story was, barely dared to take a breath. Then with a small sigh, Horace resumed his tale.

"The young man was madly in love and used to having his own way. There was no objection or social barrier that could sway his determination. He believed that he had found the love of his life — an angel in human form — and he would let nothing stand in the way of his happiness.

"Well, as you may guess, Miss Rose, the young man convinced the girl to elope, and they were married in secret. If this girl had any fault, it was only that she loved too well and yielded too easily to those who loved her. You see, she had no parents or kinfolk of her own, and her guardian was a harsh and cold man, so her young husband became the very center of her life. In the few, short months that the couple were together, they were all the world to each other.

"But it couldn't last," Horace said, and Rose could hear the deep sadness in his words. "The marriage was discovered," he continued, "and both his father and her guardian were furious. The pair were immediately separated. She was taken, with her nursemaid and housekeeper, to a plantation far from the city. And the young man was sent away to college in the North.

"Both husband and wife were devastated, as you can imagine, but they cherished the belief that they would be reunited when they both came of age and received their inheritances.

"It was not to be. Her guardian managed to intercept every letter she wrote to her young husband and every letter he wrote to her. We must suppose the old man thought he was doing right, but he deceived the girl, telling her that her absent husband had deserted her and then that he died. Imagine the cruelty of those falsehoods! The effect they had on the girl!"

Horace had risen from the bench and was rapidly pacing the ground. He wrung his hands, and Rose could see in the moonlight that his shoulders were shaking with agitation. Her impulse was to rush to him, comfort his sorrow, and beg him to forget these terrible memories. But she sat still, for she knew that Horace needed to complete his story and lay down his painful burden.

Calming himself, Horace steadied his voice and went on. "The first news that the young man received was that his wife had died just a few days after giving birth to his daughter. It seemed that nothing could help his misery. He thought he might go mad with grief and suffering. To save his sanity, he threw himself into his studies, and after a few years, the hurt he felt did lessen. But it seemed that something inside him had died along with his beautiful wife. Without her love, he grew more proud and willful than before.

"Perhaps this helps to explain why he never sought out his only child. Even when he came of age and could have taken his child from the guardian, he did nothing. In truth, he had become convinced that the child was the cause of his wife's death. It was not for a long time that he learned of the lies that were told and of his wife's desperation. For more than eight years, he blamed his poor, innocent child for his great loss, and beyond seeing that her material needs were met, he rejected her totally.

"It never occurred to him in all that time that the child had suffered a loss equal to his own, or greater, for this baby never had a chance to know her mother. It never occurred to him that the child, like the mother, might need his love and protection."

Horace stopped his pacing and looked at Rose. He could see that her eyes were glistening, but whether from tears or the moonlight, he could not tell. He went to sit beside her again, and for a moment, he laid his hand over hers.

"My story grows long," he said softly. "I will try to finish with greater speed.

"After the young man completed college, he went abroad and stayed there until his daughter was past eight years of age. Her guardian had died when she was four, and she had moved into her grandfather's home, accompanied by the housekeeper and her loyal nursemaid. The young man's only news of her came from his father and stepmother. And that lady, a jealous and twisted woman, used her letters to paint a picture of the little girl designed to poison any father's heart. The stepmother wrote of a haughty and selfish child, a self-righteous little Christian who set herself above the rest of the family and obeyed no one but herself. The stepmother's letters only confirmed the father's foolish aversion to his child. If only he had known his little girl and how anxiously she awaited his return and craved his love.

"When he at last went back to his home, he met his child with harshness and coldness, and she was so terrified of him that she could barely speak in his presence. But still she loved him, and in spite of himself, the father came to love her. Yet their troubles were not over, for he remained an arrogant and self-centered man, convinced of his own rightness and moral superiority. He had little patience with his child's strict obedience to her Christian principles. And in truth, though he would not have admitted it to himself then, he was envious of her personal relationship with her Savior. It seemed to the young man that a daughter should love and obey her father first above all.

"Well, what was inevitable happened. The daughter's unwavering obedience to God's commandments and the father's unbending demand that she obey him brought them into a conflict of wills. The father tried everything to break her will — persuasions, threats, punishments, even banishing her from his sight — but nothing could shake her faith. At last he threatened to separate her entirely from himself, to send her to a boarding school and banish her from the new home he had made ready for them. And then he left her alone in his family's home, with no one but her servant for comfort. It was too much for the poor child. Her will never broke, but her health did, and she contracted a ravaging fever that took her to the very edge of death.

Elsie's New Life

"It was only then that the father's eyes were opened. The scales fell away, and he saw how deeply he had wronged his child and his God. He repented, and for the first time in his life, he begged for the forgiveness of his Heavenly Father. And through God's great mercy, his child was saved . . . "

Horace could not go on. Tears filled his eyes, and emotion choked his throat. Rose, too, said nothing, but she reached over, and this time she took his hand in hers.

At last Horace recovered himself and said, "I have little more to tell. The child has regained her health, and she is dearer to her father's heart than words can express. Their new home is a happy place for her now, and she and her father walk the same, narrow path of love and devotion to the One who has saved them both. Only one thing is missing from their lives — the presence of a wife and mother. The father once thought he could never love again, but now he has found a gentle and kind and lovely lady who has won his heart completely. A lady who loves his daughter as she would her own."

He turned to look into Rose's eyes. "Oh, dear Rose, I've told you this story so that you will know the full truth of what I have been and what I have done. I must know now if you can trust your happiness to a man who has proved himself capable of such heartlessness?"

Rose was so overwhelmed with tender feeling that she could not speak. But Horace took her silence as rejection.

"I understand," he said in a whisper. "I was a fool to think you could love and trust me. Please, forgive my presumption. But Rose," he continued, his voice rising with the power of his emotions, "you cannot know how much you mean to me and how deeply I love you. I said that our home is happy now, but I think it will always feel empty to me if you are not there, beside me."

Rose held tighter to his hand and said, "Horace, I am afraid to say yes. I am not old enough or wise enough to become the wife and mother that you and Elsie deserve."

"You are young," Horace said, "but no one is wiser or kinder. Elsie is ready to be your daughter from this moment forward, and I think she will cause you little worry. And I — I want only to give you all the joy that a man can give. I have loved you from the moment I met you. No, even before I met you, when I read your letters to Elsie. Don't be afraid of me, Rose. Please, tell me that you will be my wife."

He stood, and he took Rose's hand and drew her up. He encircled her waist with his arm and gazed down into her face.

"I am not afraid, Horace," she said, "for 'perfect love casts out fear.' Yes, I will be your wife and Elsie's mother. For I love you both with all my heart."

And so they stood for some time in that circle of moonlight, touched by the magic warmth of love given and received and the promise of a future which they would share as one.

Elsie did not even try to go to sleep that night. Horace had left a message with Chloe to allow his daughter to stay up until he returned. (Whether the news was happy or unhappy, he wanted her to know the outcome of his conversation with Rose.)

Off and on, Elsie tried to read, but she could not focus her attention on her book. While Chloe dozed in her chair, Elsie found a piece of knitting that she had been working on. But some minutes later, after having to pull out three rows because of the stitches she had dropped, she put the project aside and tried to read again. Every now and then she went to the door, straining to hear her father's familiar footsteps. Nothing!

Each minute that passed made her more nervous. How long does it take to make a proposal, she wondered. Will Miss Rose say yes or no? She was thinking about this when the sound of the doorknob turning made her jump. And then the door opened, and there was her father, with Rose at his side. The happy looks on their faces told Elsie the whole story. She jumped up from her chair and ran to them.

"Elsie, dearest," Horace said, "I have brought you a mother. And Rose, I offer you my greatest treasure to love as I do."

Rose bent to embrace Elsie and whispered, "Are you happy, Elsie? I love you as my own, and I want you to be happy with me."

Elsie responded by hugging Rose tightly. "Oh, I am so happy, Miss Rose," she said. "I have always loved you so much."

Chloe, who had been wakened by their voices, and Horace watched this little scene with satisfaction. Then he said to his new fiancee, "Show her my token, Rose, dear."

Rose smiled and raised her left hand on which glittered a dazzling diamond ring.

"It's beautiful! But when did you get it, Papa?" Elsie asked.

"When we were in New York," he laughed. "I had only a hope then, but I decided to be prepared just in case."

Then they all laughed and talked for some minutes. Chloe, who was overjoyed at this development, shed a few tears as well. Then Rose, looking at the clock on the mantle, said that she must return to her rooms, for Edward would be returning and she wanted to tell him the news. What she didn't say was that she also wanted to avoid any chance meeting with Miss Stevens; the evening was too wonderful to be spoiled by that lady's prying.

It was hard for Horace to let Rose go, but he escorted her to her suite and bade her good-night after gaining her word that she would let him take her into breakfast the next morning.

He went back to his suite, ready to read a short passage of Scripture to Elsie and share her prayers. Chloe had gotten the little girl into bed, but when Horace entered her room, he saw immediately that Elsie had been crying.

"What is it, dear?" he asked with great concern, coming to sit beside her.

"Don't be angry, Papa. I couldn't help it."

"I'm not angry dear. Can you tell me the cause of your tears?"

"It's hard to say, Papa. I'm so happy about Miss Rose. I will have a Mamma of my own now — a Mamma who really loves me. But I'm scared, Papa, that I'll forget my first Mamma."

She pulled at the little gold chain that always hung about her neck and took the little miniature that dangled from it into her hand. "I have to look at this so often now to remember what she looked like."

Horace wrapped his strong arm around her trembling shoulders and said gently, "That's alright, my dearest. Pictures of the ones we love best often fade from our minds as time passes. But that is because they live on in our hearts, not our eyes. Your mother will always be with you, and with me. And now Rose will be with us as well. I think you are a fortunate child, Elsie, to have two mothers who love you so."

Horace could feel Elsie's trembling subside. When he looked into her face, he saw that the tears had stopped and she was smiling.

"What are you thinking now?" he asked.

"I was thinking that Annie Hart was right, Papa. She said I was to get a new mother, and she was right."

CHAPTER

9

A Surprise Over Breakfast

"Every prudent man acts out of knowledge, but a fool exposes his folly."

PROVERBS 13:16

A Surprise Over Breakfast

A number of guests had gathered in the dining room the next morning, and all but a few tables were occupied. Miss Stevens sat with several older ladies, and their conversation carried across the room.

"Where was Mr. Dinsmore last night?" one of the ladies asked, addressing her question to Miss Stevens. "He did not accompany you on your ride, I believe."

"He spent the morning riding with his daughter, and I think he was simply too fatigued for the evening's recreation," Miss Stevens replied coolly, as she cracked her boiled egg.

"He was not too fatigued for a long walk," another of the women said with a hint of mischief in her tone, "or to take a lady on his arm."

Miss Stevens looked up in surprise.

The lady lowered her voice and bent toward Miss Stevens. "You had better be on your guard, my dear," the lady said in a low whisper. "That quiet Miss Allison may prove a rival to you, for he certainly pays close attention to her."

Miss Stevens straightened, and louder than intended, she said, "That's understandable, for Mr. Dinsmore is very fond of his daughter, and this Miss Allison is obviously the child's governess. So it's natural she should accompany them whenever they ride or go walking. It is her responsibility to look after the child. But the very idea that Horace Dinsmore would look at a mere governess — no, no. He is a man of enormous pride, as is his whole family. Proud as can be."

Elsie's New Life

A gentleman at the next table, overhearing her remarks, leaned back in his chair and said, "Excuse me, but you are seriously mistaken. Miss Allison is no governess. I am well acquainted with her family, and I can assure you that her father is one of the wealthiest merchants in Philadelphia."

Miss Stevens hardly had time to register this information when there was a rustle throughout the room and all heads turned to the doorway. Horace was entering, with Rose on his arm and Elsie at his side. As they were led to their table by a waiter, all eyes seemed focused on Rose. It was little Annie Hart who blurted out what all could see: "Look, Mamma! She's wearing a diamond ring. Is it Mr. Dinsmore's ring?"

Mrs. Hart quickly hushed her daughter and then looked at Miss Stevens. That young woman, who had seen the sparkling ring before anyone else, was flushing red with rage. With as much dignity as she could summon, she rose from the table and hurriedly left the room.

Mrs. Hart followed her to the parlor and said in a sympathetic tone, "This is terrible for you, dear Miss Stevens. I understood that *you* were engaged to Mr. Dinsmore."

"Why should you think that?" Miss Stevens snapped back. "I never said so, did I?"

Mrs. Hart admitted that Miss Stevens had never said so in plain words. But she surely hinted at it, Mrs. Hart reflected to herself. All those conversations about Mr. Dinsmore's splendid new home and how Miss Stevens would alter the decor when she was mistress, and how Miss Stevens planned to change little Elsie's wardrobe when she controlled the child. Miss Stevens had repeatedly indulged in the kind of chat that was appropriate only for an engaged lady. And if Mr. Dinsmore had shown no sign of reciprocating her affections, well, everyone had assumed that it was the result of his naturally reserved and undemonstrative character. Indeed, Miss Stevens had said that very thing.

Miss Stevens plopped into a chair and burst out, "Why are people so eager to gossip? I don't care for Horace Dinsmore, and I never did! *He* has certainly paid *his* attentions to me and given me every reason to believe that *he* wanted an engagement. But *I* never encouraged his attentions, not one little bit. So now he has been captured by that scheming creature — petting and playing up to his child to curry favor with him! I thank my stars that I would never stoop to do such a thing! And if I don't miss my guess, that Miss Allison will have cause for regret soon enough. Everyone knows that Horace Dinsmore is a terrible tyrant and stubborn as a mule! I would never want *him* as a husband!"

Retreating from the young woman's tirade, Mrs. Hart thought as she left the parlor, "Those grapes are very sour, my dear girl. Very sour, indeed."

A while later, on the veranda, Annie Hart ran up to Elsie in great excitement. "Didn't I say you were going to get a new mother?" she demanded.

Elsie laughed. "Yes, you did," she replied. "But you were wrong about which mother. It is Miss Rose Allison who will be my new Mamma. And I am *very* happy, because I love her so much."

"Isn't she your governess?" Annie asked.

"No. Why do you think that?"

"Because that's what Miss Stevens said."

Before she could think, Elsie responded, "Miss Stevens says many things that aren't true."

Elsie's New Life

"Well, I'm happy for you," Annie said with a big smile. "You'll be going to a big wedding, and I bet you get a beautiful new dress, too. That will be such fun."

At that moment, Horace, Rose, and Edward came out onto the veranda, and Annie, who wanted to share her news with her mother, skipped away.

"Rose and I are going for a walk," Horace said to his beaming child. "Will you accompany us?"

"Yes, Papa. And is Mr. Edward coming?" Elsie asked, turning her bright eyes on the young man who would soon become her uncle.

"Sorry, Elsie, but I've promised to play chess with some of the ladies," Edward replied.

So Edward went his way, and the other three went theirs — across the broad lawn and onto the same path that Horace and Rose had followed the night before. Elsie chattered brightly as they walked, but both Rose and Horace were not as attentive as usual. When they came to a little bench in a clearing — a place familiar to the adults — Elsie asked if she might gather wildflowers while her father and Rose rested.

"As long as you stay within sight," her father agreed.

As Elsie tripped off to a spot some distance away, Rose spoke. "Mr. Dinsmore," she began.

"Stop there," Horace said. "If you insist on calling me 'Mr. Dinsmore', then I must address you as 'Miss Allison.' And that is no way for an engaged couple to speak. Think how the guests will talk."

Blushing a little, Rose laughed. "We are already the main topic of their conversation. But alright — Horace. I was about to say that Edward and I plan to leave tonight. It's important that I take our wonderful news to Mother and Father straightway."

A Surprise Over Breakfast

"I have beaten you to it, Rose dear. I wrote to your father this morning and had John take my letter to the train station for the first posting. Since I cannot personally request your hand, I wanted to do it by mail."

"They will be so pleased, I'm sure."

"I hate to part with you, and I won't until you set the date for our wedding. Make it soon. I must return to my home before long, and I refuse to go without you as my wife."

Rose smiled. "Will six weeks be too long? I know Mother will think even that is far too short a time to prepare for a wedding."

"A month would be better," Horace said. "The end of October."

Rose raised some objections; in particular, she worried about having an adequate wardrobe ready in just a month. But Horace easily overcame her difficulties. (In truth, Rose would have married him that very day if it did not mean robbing her mother and father of the pleasure of a large wedding.) It was soon agreed that Rose should go home to make the preparations, and meanwhile Horace and Elsie would continue their travels.

"There are still several sights left on Elsie's vacation list," Horace said, glancing at his little girl where she played. "Besides, I have some business and shopping to do in New York. We'll return there the week before the wedding, and then come to Philadelphia just before the big day. Will that suit you?"

"I will miss you," Rose replied, lowering her head, "very much. But it is a good plan. Elsie can finish her vacation, and you can escape my Mother's wedding activities. She will be in a whirl from the instant your letter arrives."

Elsie's New Life

"And I shall miss you," Horace said softly, taking her hand and pressing it to his lips.

⁓

The next month passed quickly enough, though Horace found himself counting every day. He and Elsie visited several historic sights in Connecticut and Massachusetts, then extended their journey into Canada. In a little note to Rose, Elsie wrote of her thrill at visiting her "first foreign country." Then, as Horace planned, they traveled to New York for a week of shopping. At last, they boarded the train for Philadelphia — arriving on the afternoon before the wedding.

CHAPTER

10

A Blessed Day

"Delight yourself in the Lord and he will give you the desires of your heart."

PSALMS 37:4

A Blessed Day

*E*dward Allison was standing on the train platform, wearing a broad grin. He greeted Horace and Elsie with hand-shaking and hugs and then excused himself for a few minutes. Finding John, Edward quickly gave the servant instructions about the luggage, then rushed back to where his friends stood.

"You are in high, good humor," Horace observed.

"It's a glorious occasion," Edward said as he guided them to a waiting carriage. "But I must warn you. Mother is directing this wedding as if it were a military campaign, and she, the commander-in-chief."

"And what is your rank?" Horace asked with a smile.

"I am Major Allison in charge of picking people up and getting them to the right places," Edward said as he turned to Elsie and gave her a sweeping salute. "At your service, ma'am."

Elsie laughed at his gesture, and gave him a little salute in response.

At the carriage, Edward explained, "We'll go first to the hotel where you are staying, Horace. I've directed John and Chloe to follow us with your luggage. And then you and Chloe are coming with me, Miss Elsie, to our house. I hope you don't mind sharing a room with Sophie again. Our home is quite large, but for this event, the guests are squeezed in like sardines."

Elsie was delighted to be sharing with Sophie, if it was alright with her father.

"Yes, dear," Horace said. "I can manage on my own tonight. And you will have a grand time with the ladies and girls. I know Rose is waiting to see you."

"That she is," Edward agreed. "She talks of you all the time. And I believe," he added with a grin, "that there are several other lovely ladies who are most anxious to see you."

"Who, Mr. Edward?" Elsie asked.

"Ah, let's not spoil the surprises," Edward said mysteriously. "Now into the carriage and on our way!"

When they had left Horace at the hotel, the carriage bearing Elsie, Edward, and Chloe proceeded to a lovely, tree-lined, residential neighborhood that Elsie had not seen on her previous visit to Philadelphia. The houses were large with comfortable lawns, and everything was bathed in greens and golds as the sun shown through the changing leaves of early autumn. At length, they halted in the drive of a handsome brick and stone house, and before Elsie's foot touched the ground, Sophie Allison was at her side, giggling and dancing from toe to toe.

"Oh, Elsie, can you believe it? Your Papa and my sister getting married? What fun we're going to have. Come to my room right now. You have to see my new dress for the wedding," Sophie babbled excitedly.

"You go on with Miss Sophie," Aunt Chloe told Elsie. "Take off your hat and coat, and I'll be along shortly with your things."

So Elsie and Sophie hurried into the house where the first person they saw was Mrs. Allison. The lady immediately gathered Elsie into a warm embrace. "It's so good to have you back with us, dear child," she said. "We've all missed you. And my, how pretty and healthy you look. We all want to hear about your travels, but I am so busy right now that I must leave you to Sophie's care. Rose is away at the moment, but she'll return within the hour. She wants to see you the minute she arrives."

A Blessed Day

Following Sophie, Elsie climbed the stairs and soon found herself in a charming bedroom, painted a sunny yellow just like Sophie's room at Elmgrove.

"Did your father buy you lots of dresses and pretty things in New York?" Sophie asked.

"He did, and what do you think?" Elsie replied. "He let me choose them with him. And he asked for my ideas about his clothes, too. He says that I have very good taste."

"I could have told you that," Sophie laughed. Then her little face sobered. "But can I ask you something else?" she inquired. "Are you happy that Rose will be your mother? And what will you call her?"

"Oh, Sophie, I am so happy. You know how much I love Miss Rose, and I can't imagine having a finer or kinder mother than she. And I will call her 'Mamma,' just as I call my first mother by that name, because I know Miss Rose loves me as if I were her own."

Sophie sat on the bed and a soft sigh escaped her. "I'm so glad. Rose is the best sister in the world, and I know she will be the best mother to you. I'm going to miss her a lot, you know."

"But Papa says you can come and visit us at The Oaks any time you want."

"That's right," Sophie said. "Isn't it odd, Elsie? My sister will be your mother. And your father will be my brother. What does that make you and me?"

"You will be Elsie's aunt," came a boy's voice from the doorway. The girls turned and saw Daniel standing there, a large, heavy satchel hanging from his shoulder.

"And I will be your uncle, Elsie," he continued. Dumping his bag on the floor, he moaned, "I am quite sick, you know. Sick of school."

"I thought you enjoyed your studies," Elsie said.

"Most times I do," he replied, "but not when there is a wedding underway. How can I concentrate on science and math when everyone around me is running about like wild animals?"

"Poor, poor Daniel," Sophie giggled. "Stay and talk to us for awhile."

It was not much later that a tapping at the door interrupted their conversation. Slowly the door opened, and Elsie jumped up at the sight of two beloved faces. Running to them, she was embraced from both sides by her aunts, Adelaide and Lora.

After they had all hugged and kissed several times, Adelaide took Elsie by the hand. "Come dear, someone is waiting to see you, and I have come to find you for her."

"Miss Rose?" Elsie asked expectantly.

"Who else?" her aunt replied with a loving smile.

In the dining room that night, Rose made a point of inviting Elsie to sit at her side. A few minutes later, Horace entered with Mr. Allison, who beamed with pride over the large and merry gathering of family members old and new. Behind them came Edward Allison. And with him, Elsie was delighted to see Edward Travilla. Her old friend from the South came straight to her, made a deep bow, and said, "Why, little Elsie, I see you have grown a foot since you left The Oaks. And all the roses have returned to your cheeks. I think that weddings must agree with you."

"This one does, Mr. Travilla," Elsie said happily. "Can you believe that Miss Rose will be my mother?"

"I believe that you are a most fortunate child," he responded, "to have two such loving parents to care for you."

The gentlemen then helped the ladies to their chairs, Horace seating Rose beside his daughter and taking his own place at Elsie's other side. Edward Travilla sat opposite them, between Adelaide and Lora, and all the Allisons, except the baby, arranged themselves around the commodious table.

"I am sorry that your father and his good wife could not be with us," Mrs. Allison said to Horace.

"Thank you, but my father has been ill," Horace replied.

"Not seriously, I hope," Mr. Allison interjected.

"No, sir," Horace assured. "But my stepmother wrote that she thought it would be best for him not to make the long trip." At these words, Horace cast a quick, but meaningful glance at Edward Travilla. "I know that my father will regret not being here to see you, sir, for he values your friendship greatly."

"And I his," Mr. Allison said with feeling. "Your father is a good man, Horace. You tell him that I hope to see him soon."

Supper went on in high cheer and lasted somewhat longer than usual. When the last cup and plate had been cleared, Mr. Allison called a servant to summon the household together for evening devotion. He chose as his text verses about the wedding of the Lord and His Church from the nineteenth chapter of the Book of Revelation. Everyone listened intently to the words of the Apostle John: "Then I heard what sounded like a great multitude, like the roar of rushing waters and like loud peals of thunder, shouting: 'Hallelujah! For our Lord God Almighty reigns. Let us rejoice and be glad and give him glory! For the wedding of the Lamb has come, and his bride has made herself ready. Fine linen, bright and clean, was given her to wear . . . . Blessed are those who are invited to the wedding supper of the Lamb!'"

Mrs. Allison and the servants were up and bustling before light the next morning, and Chloe came to wake Elsie and Sophie just after dawn.

"No sleepyheads this day," the nursemaid said happily as she hurried about the room, opening the drapes and gathering together the girls' clothing for the day. "Mrs. Allison wants all you children down to breakfast at seven thirty. I've got to dress you in everything 'cept your pretty dresses. You girls, wear your day dresses for now. After you eat, I'll change you and fix up your hair. I woke you early so you'd have time for your Scripture reading and prayers."

"When do we go to the church, Aunt Chloe?" Sophie asked, rubbing the sleep from her eyes.

"The carriages are gonna be here at nine o'clock, and the wedding's set to start at ten," Chloe replied. "Then you'll all come back here for the wedding breakfast. You ought to see your kitchen, Miss Sophie. Your Mamma and that cook of yours have come up with a real feast to celebrate this marriage. Now rise on up, you two."

The girls needed little encouragement. Soon they were dressed, and Chloe began packing things into Elsie's little bag.

"What are you doing, Aunt Chloe?" Sophie wanted to know. "Isn't Elsie going to stay with us?"

"Why no," Chloe said, and seeing Sophie's face fall, she added, "Miss Elsie and me and John are going with her Papa and Miss Allison — that is, she will be Mrs. Dinsmore — after the reception today. We got a train to catch if we're gonna be back at The Oaks any time soon."

"Oh, Elsie," Sophie bubbled. "You're going on a honeymoon!"

At Elsie's look of astonishment, Chloe laughed. "Not exactly, Miss Sophie. Elsie's going home with her parents because I don't expect Mr. Horace or Miss Rose can do without her."

And so the day that was to change Elsie's life began. The excited anticipation affected everyone, right down to little May and baby Daisy.

At just a few minutes before nine all the children were gathered on the driveway. Elsie and Sophie were helped into a carriage with Lora and Sophie's brothers, Richard, Daniel and Freddie. One by one, all the family and guests were loaded into their vehicles, and at last a long procession departed for the Allisons' church, where Horace and Edward Travilla, his best man, were waiting.

Elsie was seated in the very first row, next to Mrs. Allison. She saw the minister enter, and then her father and Mr. Travilla appeared. When he had taken his position, Horace looked across the pews, seeking out one little face. His eyes soon fell on Elsie, and his face lit up. Elsie had been staring at him, thinking how handsome her Papa was in his fine wedding suit. Catching his eye, she broke into a broad grin. And then her father did something he had never done before. He winked at her! Poor Elsie had to cover her mouth with her hand to keep from laughing out loud.

Elsie's New Life

The ceremony was splendid. The bride's attendants, led by Adelaide who served as maid of honor, were beautifully dressed, and Rose, who entered on her father's arm, was truly radiant.

When the vows had been exchanged, and Horace and Rose turned to greet the congregation as husband and wife, the happiness in their faces was almost breathtaking. Even Mrs. Allison, who had wept silently throughout the ceremony, emitted a gasp, and Elsie had a sense that the whole church had suddenly become a little brighter.

❦

The wedding breakfast extended well into the afternoon, as the house full of guests celebrated the union of Horace Dinsmore and Rose Allison. Mrs. Allison wavered between smiles and tears, for parting with her eldest daughter was the saddest occasion she had experienced. She comforted herself, however, with the knowledge that Horace's love for Rose was both tender and true. And she reminded herself each time she glimpsed Elsie's curly head in the crowd of guests that she had not lost a daughter, but gained a granddaughter. So the dear lady's tears gradually subsided, and her smiles won the day.

After several hours, Adelaide sought out Elsie.

"Your Papa sent me to tell you that it's time to change your dress, little birdie," Adelaide said. "Your train back to the South will be leaving in an hour, and Rose has already gone to her room to change into her traveling outfit. Chloe is waiting for you right now."

Elsie nodded and started to walk away, but Adelaide took her hand. "Are you very happy, little one?" the young woman asked.

"Very," Elsie replied softly. "I think I will always be happy now, with Papa and my new Mamma to love me and watch over me."

For a moment, Adelaide's eyes became misty. She had seen Elsie weather so many storms in her young life. She had nursed the child through the worst moments of illness. And she had learned from Elsie the full power of their Lord and Savior's love. Feeling the depth of Elsie's joy on this day, Adelaide raised a quick, silent prayer of gratitude to the Lord.

Recovering her smile, Adelaide gave Elsie a gentle push toward the stairway. "Hurry upstairs, pet," Adelaide said, "You have a long journey to take with your Papa and Mamma, and you don't want to be late."

CHAPTER

Time and Changes

"Oh, the depth of the riches of the wisdom and knowledge of God! How unsearchable his judgments, and his paths beyond tracing out!"

ROMANS 11:33

$\mathcal{E}$lsie had turned eleven in the summer that she regained her health and her father fell in love with Miss Rose Allison. And from that season forward, her young life was never the same. Encouraged by Horace, Rose became "Mamma" in every sense of the word — loving, teaching, comforting, and when necessary (which wasn't very often) disciplining. She loved Elsie, but Rose also accepted her motherly responsibility to guide her new daughter along God's path and protect her from too much indulgence and pampering. Both Horace and Elsie quickly learned to trust Rose's opinion and counsel in everything; as Horace was fond of saying, Rose was wise beyond her years and blessed with more good sense than most people of twice her age and life experience.

When they had all settled into comfortable routines back at The Oaks, Elsie and her Papa and Mamma became that remarkable and wonderful thing — a family. Wrapped in the security of her parents' love, Elsie felt that her life was complete. But more change was coming. About a year and a half after Rose and Horace's marriage, the happy couple presented Elsie with a gift she had often longed for — a brother. The baby, named Horace like his father and grandfather, was a bright-eyed and robust little thing who captured Elsie's heart the moment she first beheld him. Far from feeling jealous, as many children naturally do when a new child arrives, Elsie adored her brother and took great delight in helping her Mamma to care for the baby. And it was Elsie who gave the boy his nickname.

One evening when the infant was about three months old, Elsie was in the library with her father. Horace was reading, and she was working on a difficult set of math problems when an idea suddenly struck her.

"There are now three Horaces in our family, Papa," she commented.

"That there are, dearest," Horace replied, "and honored as I am that my son bears my name, I fear we may face some confusion when he grows older. Shall all of us appear whenever anyone calls for 'Horace'? If your Mamma says, 'Horace, drink your milk' or 'Horace, get out of the mud,' how will I know that she is not speaking to me or even your grandfather if he happens to be visiting?"

Elsie giggled at the image of her father and grandfather playing in mud. Then she asked, "What were you called when you were a boy at Roselands?"

Horace laid down the book he was reading, and a soft smile of remembrance came to his face. "Before she died," he said, "my mother always called me 'little Horace.' And there were servants and friends who called me by that name even when I had reached almost six feet in height. Most people addressed me as 'Horace, Junior,' and that's how my father usually referred to me. I guess I must refer to my son as 'Horace the Third,' although that makes him sound more like an old English king than our precious little boy."

"I have an idea, Papa. Three Horaces is a triple," Elsie noted. "So do you think I could call him 'Trip'? He will always be Horace the Third, but 'Trip' seems like a good name for a little boy."

Horace was thoughtful. He tried the nickname aloud several times and then said, "It just might do, Elsie. But we

must see what your Mamma thinks about it. She may not approve of turning her little gentleman into a 'Trip.'"

Rose, however, thought the name charming. So thanks to his sister, little Horace Dinsmore the Third was soon known as "Trip" to everyone who loved him.

Over the next three years, little Trip grew from a gurgling babe into an energetic and curious toddler who loved to run and explore, leading his entire family on a merry chase each day. Horace acquired a few more gray hairs, but otherwise he and Rose maintained their youthful looks and generous ways. And as she grew toward womanhood, Elsie came more and more to resemble her own dear mother — the first Elsie — both in appearance and in temperament. She bloomed like a rose, though she seemed hardly aware of her beauty. She continued to be her father's devoted student, studying increasingly difficult subjects under his tutelage. Horace also oversaw her riding lessons, and much to his pleasure, she developed into a skilled and fearless horsewoman. Rose became her chief teacher in the domestic arts, and excellent tutors rode out from the city each week to continue her piano and singing lessons.

It was a busy life for a young girl, yet almost never a day passed that Elsie did not have her prayer and devotion time. With both Rose and Horace to share and guide her study of the Scriptures, Elsie's spiritual understanding matured, and though it hardly seemed possible, her faith in and love for the Lord deepened.

Not many miles away, changes were also taking place at Roselands. Although Adelaide remained at home, first

Elsie's New Life

Louise and then Lora married. Louise's new husband was a businessman, and after their wedding, the couple returned to his home state far from the South. Lora was not so distant from her family, however. To everyone's delight, she had wed the Howards' eldest son, Charles, and they now resided at Tinegrove, his parents' nearby plantation.

Miss Day, the governess, departed Roselands when Enna was the last child left in the schoolroom, and Enna's education became Adelaide's task — by no means an easy one, given Enna's spoiled and flighty ways. Walter, still the most shy and bookish of the Dinsmore children, would soon be leaving the family home to enter college in the North. There he would share rooms with his brother Arthur.

And what of Arthur? He had completed his boarding school with only a few troublesome incidents on his record. During his summer vacations at Roselands, he was cooperative and obedient under his father's ever-watchful eye. Arthur entered the same prestigious university which Horace had attended, and while his performance there was not outstanding, it was satisfactory. With sighs of relief, everyone began to believe that the hostile and guileful boy had truly mended his ways and was growing into a responsible young man.

The elder Mr. Dinsmore and his wife were aging well enough, though Mrs. Dinsmore seemed incapable of softening with time. In fact, she became more ill-humored and critical of others with each passing year. The senior Mr. Dinsmore, however, found a new pleasure in his grandson and was a frequent visitor at The Oaks. He had grown somewhat kinder to Elsie, but it was little Trip upon whom he doted. Horace and Rose often worried that her grandfather's obvious favoritism would cause Elsie pain. But Elsie felt no disappointment; instinctively she understood that pride was the cause of her grandfather's indifferent affection for her. He had wronged her when she lived under his roof, and he could not bring himself to admit it. She prayed for him, asking that he might come to know the boundless love and forgiveness of Jesus. And she forgave him, just as she forgave Arthur and the others who had treated her so thoughtlessly.

One summer afternoon several months before her sixteenth birthday, Elsie was out riding with Jim as her diligent companion. (Jim had grown up, too, and become Horace's head stable man, but he never gave up his role as Elsie's guardian when Horace was not present.)

Elsie asked if they had time to go to Tinegrove before returning for supper.

"I believe so, Miss Elsie," Jim replied, taking note of the sun's position. "But it's got to be a short visit if you want to get back by the time the cook rings the supper bell."

The sun was still high when Elsie arrived at the Howards' splendid mansion, and she found everyone except Charles Howard at home. After greeting the elder Mr. and Mrs. Howard, she hurried to Lora's sitting room where her young aunt and Carrie Howard were busy with their sewing needles, mending a large pile of sheets and pillow cases.

The three had not been together for several weeks and had much to talk about, but when at length Carrie asked Elsie to stay for supper, Elsie suddenly realized how much time had passed.

"I'm sorry," she said, reaching for her riding hat and her scarf. "I must be going. It's getting late, and Papa never wants me out after sunset unless he's riding with me."

"Are you sure you can't stay?" Carrie asked.

"Don't beg her," Lora said with a little laugh. "I know my brother, and Elsie's right. Horace will be worried if she is late." Taking Elsie's arm to walk her to the door, Lora added, "Some say that Horace is overprotective of you, but he always errs on the right side. Promise to come see us again soon, Elsie."

"Yes," Carrie said as Elsie mounted her horse. "But come early next time, so you may stay longer."

Elsie and Jim cantered their horses most of the way back to The Oaks, reining them in when they reached the gates of home.

"We've made it, Jim," Elsie declared.

"With a few minutes to spare, Miss Elsie," the servant responded. "But a very few."

Elsie settled her horse, Glossy, into a comfortable walk and proceeded up the drive. Immediately she caught sight of a tall figure walking toward her, and at first she thought it was her father. But by the man's slouching gait, she realized that it was in reality her uncle Arthur. As she came close to him, he reached out and seized Glossy's bridle.

"Stay a moment, Elsie," he said, holding the horse still. "I want to speak to you."

"Then come into the house, and we can talk there," she said. "I'm late, and Papa will be wondering where I am."

"No," Arthur said emphatically. Then softening his tone, he went on, "I won't detain you but for a minute or two." He turned to Elsie's companion and ordered, "You ride ahead, Jim. I want to speak to Miss Elsie in private."

Reluctantly, Jim walked his horse farther along the drive, out of earshot but not out of sight.

"I need a favor from you," Arthur said when he was sure Jim could not overhear. "I want to borrow a little money. It's just a trifle — fifty dollars or so — and I will repay you in a couple of weeks. Will you accommodate me?"

"I'll be glad to, Arthur, but not without Papa's knowledge and permission. I hope you don't want to conceal this matter from him."

"I see no reason why he should know about my private affairs. Besides, you're old enough to do as you like with your own money."

"But I'm not, Arthur. I must account to Papa each month for every cent I spend, so he will know about a loan whether you tell him or not."

"Then you can give it to me now, and I'll repay it before the end of the month. He'll never know."

"But he will know," Elsie said firmly, "because I'll tell him. We have been through this before, Arthur, and you know that I will not keep secrets from Papa. But I'll be glad to make you the loan if you will tell Papa about it. Come up to the house, and we can talk to him now. You can tell him how much you need and what it is for."

Arthur was becoming desperate, and his voice rose in anger. "Never!" he shouted. "You were always the most selfish and disobliging girl, Elsie. And you haven't changed one bit."

"Then let go of my horse," she returned. "I'm late, and I must get home."

"Go on then," he said in a voice that was now icy with his fury. "I should have known that I could not find help from you."

Elsie's New Life

Muttering something under his breath, Arthur released the bridle. But as Elsie guided the horse away from him, Arthur raised a small stick that he had been holding and struck the horse with a stinging blow on its flank.

From where he sat, Jim could not see Arthur's action. But he watched in horror as Elsie's terrified horse shied, then reared on her hind legs and plunged down again. Startled, Elsie nevertheless managed to hang on, and as Glossy bolted forward, she struggled to regain the reins. Reacting almost instantly, Jim raced toward her. Reversing his own steed's direction to bring it alongside Glossy, Jim was able to grab the loose reins in his strong hands. "Whoa! Whoa there. Steady on!" he exclaimed as he pulled Glossy up.

When both horses had come to a halt, Elsie jumped down from her saddle and gently began to soothe her frightened mare. Stroking Glossy's head and wet neck, Elsie crooned, "There, there girl. Steady now, Glossy. My pretty Glossy. No one will harm you now. No one will ever harm you again so long as I am your mistress."

Inside Elsie boiled with anger, but she kept her voice silky smooth until Glossy was calm again. Then she handed the reins to Jim, who had alighted from his horse.

"I'll walk from here, Jim," she said. "Will you take Glossy to the stables and cool her down for me?"

"I sure will, Miss Elsie. And don't you worry 'bout her now. She just got a fright." Jim wanted to ask what had happened, although he was very sure who had caused Glossy to buck and run. But Elsie was already walking up the long drive, and the last rays of sunlight were fading fast.

Several minutes later, Horace, who had been standing on the front steps, saw his daughter approaching and hurried forward to meet her.

"Where is Glossy?" he asked. "Why are you on foot, dear Daughter? Where's Jim?"

"We were late, Papa, so I had Jim take the horses directly to the stable," she replied. "I'm so sorry if I worried you. I rode to Tinegrove, to see Lora and Carrie, and we were having such a good visit that I lost track of the time."

"Well," Horace said, "I can excuse you this once, but don't let it happen again. Your Mamma and I cannot help becoming anxious about you."

"I know, Papa. And I never want to worry you or Mamma."

Horace draped his arm around her shoulder, and they walked back to the house. Running toward them was a small, curly-headed boy who shouted happily, "Elsie's home! Elsie's home!" And behind him, Rose walked up to greet her daughter.

Giving Elsie one more quick hug, Horace then bent forward to catch his son in his arms, sweeping the laughing boy high into the air and then onto his own broad shoulders.

"I believe I am the most fortunate of men," Horace said, his face lit with a smile that brightened even the dusky end of the day.

In her room, as Aunt Chloe quickly helped her change from her black riding clothes into a neat, white muslin frock, Elsie considered the events of that afternoon.

What is Arthur up to, she asked herself. Had all the reports of his improved behavior been false? Should she tell her father about Arthur's request for money and his cruel treatment of Glossy? She considered this question carefully. Elsie never told her father falsehoods, but there were times when she did not confide everything to him. She was deeply angry at Arthur for his treatment of her horse, but she knew that her father would think only of the possible danger to her. But she had not been in any real jeopardy, not with Jim so close by. She would have told Horace everything that happened if the fault had been hers, but this was different; she had done nothing wrong. Besides, the thing was over and done now. So why should she cause her Papa to worry when it was not necessary? "Arthur must know by now that I won't help him against Papa's wishes," she told herself. "This will be the end of it, I'm quite sure. Whatever Arthur does, he won't trouble me again."

Feeling confident that her decision was the right one, Elsie put the whole affair into the back of her mind and went to join her parents in the dining room. To her delight, Edward Travilla was there as well.

"I have brought you something," he said, greeting her with a sly smile. "But I shall enjoy a good meal before I present it to you."

"Oh, please, Mr. Travilla, won't you give me a hint?" Elsie begged.

"Not even a little one," he replied as he helped her to her seat.

When everyone adjourned to the parlor after supper, Edward took a package wrapped in paper from the table where he had left it and placed it in Elsie's hands.

By its shape and weight, Elsie guessed the contents. "A book," she said excitedly. "Oh, Mr. Travilla, you know I love books better than silver and gold."

"In that and so much more, you are your father's child," Edward responded. "Now open it. I have already received your father's approval of its contents."

To be sure, Elsie looked quickly toward her Papa. At his nod, she removed the wrapping and found a brand new book, its spine not yet cracked.

"Oh, it is by Mr. Charles Dickens," she said with enthusiasm. She read the title, *"David Copperfield."*

"It's his newest novel, Elsie. Your Papa reminded me recently how much you enjoyed Mr. Dickens's writing, so I ordered this one sent from London."

Remembering her manners, Elsie said, "Thank you so much, Mr. Travilla! I do like Mr. Dickens very much, though I've only read a couple of his books. Papa and Mamma and I have read *A Christmas Carol* aloud several times and enjoyed it every time."

"Now that is a book with a happy ending," Horace said, "and a message we might all take into account. Old Scrooge shows us that even a man with the meanest spirit may open his eyes and his heart and redeem himself in time."

"May I begin reading this now, Papa?" Elsie asked.

"Yes, dear. Edward and I are going to talk for awhile in the library, and your Mamma must get Trip into his bed. You'll have this room to yourself."

Elsie was soon engrossed in the story of poor little David Copperfield and his sufferings, and the memory of her brush with Arthur vanished completely from her head. So involved was she in the story that she was oblivious to the time until she felt a gentle hand on her shoulder.

"Come, dear," Horace said. "The servants have gathered for our devotions."

Elsie's New Life

Marking her place in the book, Elsie rose quickly and followed her father. "Has Mr. Travilla gone?" she asked.

"He has, just minutes ago."

"I wanted to thank him again for his gift," Elsie said with a disappointed little sigh. "He was so kind to think of me."

"You must ask Edward to tell you about the time he met Charles Dickens," Horace said, piquing Elsie's curiosity. "It was a number of years ago, just before I had come home from Europe, I believe. Mr. Dickens was on a tour of our country, and Edward heard him deliver a talk and then met him personally."

"How exciting! To meet a real, famous author," Elsie exclaimed as they entered the dining room where all but the littlest were gathered.

"To be sure," Horace replied. "But there is no author so great as our Precious Lord, nor any book so full of love and truth as the one we will read now."

Then taking a worn little Bible from his pocket, Horace turned to the passage he had selected for that evening's devotion and began to read.

A Friend to the Rescue

"For the Lord gives wisdom, and from his mouth come knowledge and understanding.... He is a shield to those whose walk is blameless, for he guards the course of the just and protects the way of his faithful ones."

PROVERBS 2:6-8

A Friend to the Rescue

*T*t was several days later. And had anyone been looking, they would have been surprised to see a slim and attractive girl moving quietly along the gravel path that encircled The Oaks. At each window, the little figure paused and peered inside, then shook her head and moved on. When she came to a set of glass doors that opened onto a small porch at the side of the house, she stopped. Planting her hands firmly on her hips and cocking her head sideways, she announced to the doors, "Well, I might have known. Buried under a pile of books and happy as a clam!"

At these words, Elsie's voice rang out from the sitting room. "Why, Lucy Carrington! How did you get here?"

Lucy entered the room and made a low curtsey. "I hope my lady will excuse this intrusion upon her studies," she said with mock gravity, "but I have ridden over from yonder Ashlands to rescue you from your labors. I promise never again to interrupt the Lady Elsie, until the next time."

Both girls laughed merrily, and Elsie guided her friend to a comfortable chair. "But Lucy, shouldn't you be hard at your books as well?" she asked.

"I am on vacation," Lucy said with a fresh laugh. "At least my governess is. Miss Warren has gone to see her family, and her poor little student is left behind with a whole week free of books and lessons."

"I'm sure Papa will be glad to include you in our studies," Elsie said with a smile.

Lucy threw up her hands. "Horrors! I should die of fright the first time he asked me to recite. And anyway, I have a much better suggestion. You must come stay with me and cheer me up. Mamma has sent me to invite you to Ashlands for the week, and everyone wants you to come, especially Herbert."

"How is he?" Elsie asked with concern. Herbert was Lucy's twin brother, and for as long as Elsie had known him, he had suffered terribly from a hip condition that sapped his strength and often caused great pain.

"Oh, he is sometimes better and sometimes worse," Lucy said, a look of worry clouding her pretty face. "The doctor is doing his best, but I wish there were something I could do for him." Then her face cleared, and she said, "But I can. I can convince you to visit us, for you are always a tonic to Herbert. No one can lift his spirits as you do. Won't you come home with me?"

"I do want to," Elsie replied, "if Papa says I may."

"Then let's go and ask him now," Lucy said, rising from her chair.

"But he's away on business today and won't return until supper time."

Undaunted, Lucy said, "Then we will ask your Mamma. Can't she give you permission just as well?"

"Not for such a long visit," Elsie explained. "If I am to be away for a week, she and Papa must decide together."

"Oh, pooh," Lucy said with a pout. "Your Papa is the strictest man alive. If I were you, I would always be in trouble, for I am too used to having my own way."

"You exaggerate so much," Elsie said. "I know that you obey your Mamma and Papa as I do mine."

"Yes," Lucy agreed, "but my Mamma and Papa usually let me do as I like. I'm really not half as good as you."

Elsie laughed. "And I am not half so good as you like to think," she said. "So there. We are even."

A Friend to the Rescue

Lucy looked doubtful, but she said, "Be that as it may, do you think your Papa will permit you to visit? You can come tomorrow if he agrees."

"I'm not sure he will want me to leave my studies for an entire week," Elsie replied.

"But we won't be wholly idle. We will practice piano every day and maybe learn some duets. And Mamma and Grandmamma will help us with our sewing. And we'll read together — Herbert will love that. And I have a special reason for wanting you to come. Have you forgotten? It is Herbert's and my birthday at the weekend, and Mamma is planning ever such a nice party. Not a big one, but Carrie is invited, and Enna and Mary Leslie and some more of the boys and girls we've grown up with. You must come, Elsie, and help with the preparations. Please say you will. After all, it's not every day that we turn sixteen."

Elsie did want to go, so she said, "Just let me ask Papa tonight, and I'm sure he will say yes."

"I would advise you to coax him, except that I know it would do no good at all," Lucy said with a wry smile. "But try your best, Elsie, and I will be looking for you and Aunt Chloe to arrive tomorrow." She was heading to the door and said, "If I can't take you with me, I really have to be going. Mamma told me not to stay too long."

Elsie hugged her friend and said, "See there, Lucy, you are not nearly so disobedient as you pretend. I promise to speak to Papa the minute he returns. I'm sure he will want me to be there for your sixteenth. But if there is a problem, I will send a message by Jim."

"And I'll cross my fingers and my toes until I see you," Lucy laughed as she ran across the porch to the path that would take her back to her horse.

Elsie's New Life

Elsie finished her lessons, and after dinner, she retreated to a special place in the garden that she had made her own. Nestled on a terraced hillside, the grassy spot offered a splendid view of the river that bordered her father's property. Except in the hottest part of summer, clean, fresh breezes always seemed to blow on the hill, sometimes carrying the aroma of the distant sea. In the middle of the clearing sat a wooden arbor over which rose vines grew in profusion. There was a bench under the little arbor, and nearby stood an old, bronze pedestal that supported a sundial. Elsie loved this place and had adopted it for herself soon after moving to The Oaks. Whenever her parents or any of the servants wished to find her, they always thought first of "Elsie's Arbor," and so the place acquired its name.

Today, she had gone there to read her new book, and with her imagination wholly captivated by the tribulations of young David Copperfield, she didn't hear approaching footsteps.

When something tugged hard at her hair, she jumped in pain rather than fright and looked up to see Arthur bending over her.

"I suppose you're going to cry now," he said with a sneer.

"Why should I?" she asked impatiently.

But Arthur ignored her question to ask one of his own: "What are you reading there? Some namby-pamby little girl's story, I suppose. Or maybe it's something that Horace wouldn't approve of, and you've sneaked up here to read it in secret."

Elsie was shocked at the idea. "Only you would think that, Arthur," she said in disgust. "It's the new book by Charles Dickens, and Papa approves of it thoroughly."

"Too bad," he said. "If you'd been trying to get away with something, I'd have you in my power."

"How?"

"Because I might have to tell your dear Papa all about it, unless you did as I said. I know how afraid you are of Horace — scared to death of him."

Elsie's face reddened, and she burst out, "I am not! I obey Papa because I love him."

Laughing nastily, Arthur pointed a finger just inches from her face and shouted, "You look like a beet, Elsie! A bright red beet! Why are you so mad? Where is all your Christian spirit now, little girl?"

His taunt cut her, and she tried mightily to compose herself. But Arthur would not cease his cruel teasing. Once more he grabbed her hair and pulled hard. "Don't you wish I'd go away? Don't you just wish I'd leave you alone."

"You are right about that. I don't understand why you're always so rude to me, but since you are and nothing I do ever helps, then I shall go away." At that, Elsie stood up and would have walked off except that Arthur grasped her wrist and held it tightly.

"Not so easily done, Miss Prissy. You can go just as soon as you do as I say. I want that money I asked for the other day, and I want it now!"

"No. Not unless you tell Papa what you want it for," Elsie said in as calm a voice as she could muster. "That was my answer before, and it will always be my answer."

This time, it was Arthur's face that glowed red. He twisted his grip on Elsie's wrist, making her wince. "You are as rich as old King Croesus," he hissed, "and too mean to lend me a paltry fifty dollars. What is wrong with you? Why, you're fifteen, almost sixteen years old, and you're too much of a coward to do what you like with your own money. Will you let Horace lead you around for all your life, like a puppy dog on a leash? Don't you have an ounce of spirit in you? Will you always be no better than a sniveling little baby?"

Against her will, the tears now rushed from Elsie's eyes — hot tears of rage at his words. Her throat was so choked she couldn't speak, but she pulled away, trying without success to free herself from his grasp.

"You will give me that money!" Arthur demanded again, but Elsie shouted back at him. "Never! After what you said, I'll never give in to you!"

As her words came out, she saw Arthur's expression change. His eyes grew dark and wild, and all the color drained from his face. His lips stretched wide and white in a terrifying mockery of a smile. And Elsie was suddenly conscious of his free hand, raised above his head, ready to strike down on her.

She closed her eyes and screamed. And he let go of her wrist. She kept her eyes squeezed shut and raised her arms to ward off the expected blow. Instead, she heard a loud grunt, followed by an agonized groan. And before she looked, she knew that Arthur was no longer standing over her.

When she opened her eyes, she saw him on the ground, nursing his own arm now and trying to retreat from the tall figure who stood over him.

It was Edward Travilla, and as he advanced on Arthur, he spoke in tones so low and hard that Elsie barely recognized his voice.

A Friend to the Rescue

"You are the lowest kind of coward," Edward said to the groveling young man at his feet. "To strike a girl — that is the act of a spineless bully and unworthy of any man who carries the Dinsmore name."

Frightened as he was, Arthur could not restrain his tongue. "I have every right to strike her, Travilla," he cried out. "I am her uncle, and I may discipline her as I please."

Edward straightened to his full height. His face was turned away from Elsie, but she could see that his right hand was tightening around the handle of the riding crop he held at his side.

"Please don't hit him, Mr. Travilla!" she cried out.

Without taking his gaze off Arthur, Edward replied, "I have no intention of wasting a blow on him, Elsie. He is no better than a worm and not worth my efforts." Hearing these words, Arthur began slowly to struggle to his feet. But Edward took a step forward, and Arthur froze.

"I warn you now, Arthur," Edward said in a voice that seemed to be forged of iron. "If you ever again raise a hand to Elsie, or any woman or girl, I shall not let you go a second time. And I promise that should you even attempt to threaten your niece again, you will live to regret it. Get up and go. Now!"

Trembling and fearing she might faint, Elsie had taken her seat under the bower and lowered her head into her hands. When Edward next spoke to her, it was in the warm tones she was accustomed to, and the mere sound seemed to calm her shaking. She raised her eyes and was immediately aware that Arthur was no longer present.

"Are you all right, child?" Edward asked. "Did he hurt you in any way?"

"No, sir," she said, not wanting to mention the stinging pain at her wrist. "He just frightened me, and I don't understand why he is so angry with me."

"Tell me what happened. Perhaps I can find a reason," Edward encouraged. So Elsie told him the whole story, including the events of the other day when Arthur had so abused her horse. When she finished, she asked, "Must you tell Papa? I don't know what he will do to Arthur if he knows."

"I think I must tell him, dear girl, for Horace is your father and he has the right to know. But don't worry about that now. I see you have your new book here. Tell me your opinion of what you have read thus far."

In this way, Edward helped Elsie recover from the terrible scene with Arthur. They talked of the book, and Edward related in detail the story of his meeting with Mr. Dickens, much to Elsie's delight. After about a half hour, she seemed to have fully recovered her sunny self, and Edward suggested that he walk her back to the house before making his departure. (In fact, Edward was fearful that Arthur might not have departed the grounds, and he intended to maintain his guard over Elsie until he could entrust her to Horace's care.)

Horace was just dismounting his horse when they walked up to the house. Elsie ran to him, her face aglow with a happy smile, and he hugged her warmly, then greeted his old friend.

"Edward, can you stay for supper?" Horace asked.

"Not tonight, for my mother has a guest coming," Edward replied. "But I'll return tomorrow, for there is a matter I wish to discuss."

"Is it urgent?" Horace wondered.

A Friend to the Rescue

"Tomorrow will do, I think," Edward said, untying his own horse from the nearby post. When he had ridden around the first curve in the drive — out of the sight of Horace and his daughter — Edward turned his horse away from the graveled roadway. He intended to do some scouting among the wooded areas of Horace's estate before the light faded.

Before supper, Elsie had a short lesson with her father, reciting her texts for the day to perfection. She intended to tell him then of Lucy's invitation, but before she could begin, Horace said, "I have something serious to discuss with you, dearest. I must ask if you have lent any money to Arthur lately."

The question took her by surprise, but she responded in all honesty, "No, Papa. You told me never to give him money without your knowledge and permission. I wouldn't disobey you."

Horace smiled a little. "I know you would not, but it has been a long while since I gave you that command, and I would understand if you had forgotten. The truth is that your grandfather and I are very worried about Arthur. The boy is clever and has hidden much of the wrongs he has done, but enough has come to light to disturb your grandfather. He believes that Arthur has not changed his old habits, and we fear that he may be gambling again, so you can see why it is important that he not receive money from any of us."

"Poor Grandpapa," Elsie said.

"Yes," Horace agreed. "I was at Roselands today, and my father seems to have aged years in just the past few weeks.

For his sake, I will be glad when fall comes and Arthur returns to school. Walter will be with him this year, and perhaps his presence will be a healthy influence."

"Oh, I hope so, Papa," Elsie said fervently. "Walter is a good boy. But Papa, we must pray for Arthur, that God will change his heart."

"Yes, dear, let us do that now. Let us agree together to ask Him to do His great work, for I fear there is no human power to save Arthur now."

And so they prayed, and when their prayer was done, they sat in silence for some minutes, until they heard the ringing of the supper bell. It was only at that moment that Elsie remembered her original intention. Quickly she told her father of Lucy's visit that morning and the invitation to visit Ashlands.

Horace caught her by surprise once again. "I think that is a splendid idea, Daughter. You have done so well in your studies that a little vacation seems in order. I doubt that a week of fun will hurt a scholar such as you. I'm sure you will be helpful to Mrs. Carrington and Lucy with the party preparations. And more important, I think your presence will be most welcome to young Herbert. That poor boy has endured so much, and we should give him whatever joy we can."

"And you will not miss me, Papa?" Elsie asked.

"Of course, I will, Elsie dear," he said with a deep laugh, "but I can spare you for a few days for a good cause. And your Mamma will agree, I'm certain, although your little brother might put up an argument. Luckily, he does not have a vote in this decision."

CHAPTER

Welcome Guests and Unwanted Visitors

"Wisdom will save you from the ways of wicked men, from men whose words are perverse, who leave the straight paths to walk in dark ways, who delight in doing wrong and rejoice in the perverseness of evil, whose paths are crooked and who are devious in their ways."

PROVERBS 2:12-15

*B*ut are you absolutely sure she'll come?" Herbert asked. "What time is it?" He was sitting on a sofa on the terrace of his family's fine plantation house, shaded from the warm sun under bowers of wisteria.

His sister heaved an exasperated sigh and looked at her little watch. "It is two minutes later than the last time you asked. Just after ten o'clock. And no, I'm not *absolutely* sure she will come. I am not *absolutely* sure of anything. But I do believe she will come," Lucy said, the irritation gone from her tone. "And we have received no message from The Oaks this morning. She said she'd send a message if she couldn't come."

"That's a good sign, I suppose," Herbert said. He picked up the book he was reading and tried to focus on the story. But within a minute he was looking up toward the drive again, hoping to see a carriage or a horse coming toward the house.

Harry Carrington, one of the twins' older brothers, walked out onto the terrace and in a jolly manner asked, "What do you say to a game of chess, Herbert?"

"He's too fidgety for chess," Lucy volunteered. "We're watching for Elsie to arrive, and Herbert is nervous that she won't be able to come."

"Can't blame you, old man," Harry said lightly to his brother. "It's always a treat to have Elsie around the house. But look out! I see someone riding up the drive. I do believe it's a pretty girl on a black horse."

"It's Elsie!" the twins cried out in happy unison. And both Lucy and Harry rushed off to meet their friend.

Elsie's New Life

Herbert looked down at a little servant boy who had been playing jacks nearby. "Archie, will you please fetch me my crutch and cane?" The little boy jumped up and ran to get the requested items. "What a bother it is to be a cripple," Herbert said to himself as he watched the child.

But before little Archie could help Herbert to his feet, a sweet voice rang out, "Don't get up for me, Herbert," and then Elsie was there, extending her hand to her dear friend and inquiring about his health.

"I'm not too bad," Herbert replied, "though my leg is not so strong as it should be. But my doctor is a determined man, and he says we will conquer this disease yet."

"I pray for that," Elsie said as she took a seat in the chair next to Herbert's couch. "You are always so brave."

"That he is," agreed Lucy who had accompanied her friend onto the terrace. "And your visit will do him a world of good, I know." Lucy didn't seem to notice the blush that came to Herbert's face at her words; she went on chatting with Elsie and her brother for a few minutes and finally said, "We'll have plenty of time for talk later. Elsie, I'll take you upstairs to see Mamma and my grandparents. I'm sure Aunt Chloe will be along presently, and Harry will see that your luggage is taken up to the guest room."

Elsie cast a glance toward the drive and saw the cart from The Oaks lumbering toward the house, her nursemaid sitting in the front with the driver. "Yes, there's Aunt Chloe now. Will you excuse us, Herbert, while we go to see your mother?"

"Of course," Herbert replied politely. "I will still be here when you return."

So the two girls, linked arm-in-arm, walked into the house together, and Herbert followed their progress, though in truth his eyes were focused on only one.

After greeting Mrs. Carrington, who nearly smothered her with hugs and kisses, and Mr. and Mrs. Norris, Lucy's grandparents, the girls retreated to a lovely bedroom on the second floor. Everything was in place, waiting for the guest. Bouquets of fresh summer flowers — arranged by Lucy that very morning — had been placed on the mantle, and their soft fragrances filled the room.

Aunt Chloe soon arrived, and while she unpacked the bags and helped Elsie change from her riding habit into a charming summer dress, the girls talked of their plans for the week.

"Shall we go back to join Herbert?" Elsie asked. "I have brought something I think will interest him."

"What is it?" Lucy asked as Elsie took an object from one of her cases. "I see. A book. I hope it is an interesting one, for you know I'm not much of a bookworm."

Elsie laughed. "I'm sure you will enjoy this. I haven't got very far in it yet, but it is a great adventure."

"Well, Herbert is sure to be pleased. I sometimes think books are his best friends. Come, let's show him what you have."

Herbert was still on the terrace as he said he would be. He was working on a small piece of wood with his knife, and tiny chips lay scattered around him on the terrace floor. So often confined to couch or bed, Herbert had taken up carving several years earlier as a way to pass the time when he grew tired of reading. He had begun by making little boxes and simple whistles; now he concentrated on intricately detailed birds that were nearly perfect miniatures of the creatures who made their homes in the trees of Ashlands.

"What is that to be?" Elsie asked as she took the chair at Herbert's side.

Elsie's New Life

"It's going to be a bluebird," he said, "though it is only a chunk of wood at the moment. Perhaps I can finish it while you're here."

"Oh, I hope so," Elsie replied with enthusiasm. "I don't know how you do it, Herbert. It's as if you were making magic in your hands."

Blushing slightly, Herbert said, "Carving keeps me occupied."

"Elsie has brought us a book to read," Lucy said gaily.

Elsie held out the volume she carried, and Herbert took it. "The new Dickens," he said. "How exciting. Have you read it yet, Elsie?"

"Just a bit. I thought we might start over and read it together, from the beginning."

"That will be great fun. I do enjoy Mr. Dickens's tales. Have you read many of them, Elsie?"

"Only *A Christmas Carol* and *Nicholas Nickleby*, and this new one. Papa says that I am old enough to understand his books now."

"I'm glad *you* understand books," Lucy hooted. "Whatever I read seems to fly out of my head quicker than the birds Herbert copies."

"That's because you won't concentrate your mind," Herbert said a little peevishly. "You have a perfectly good mind, Lucy. You just fill it with useless things."

"Like plans for our birthday party, dear brother?" Lucy teased.

"Well," Herbert said slowly, "I guess that is important. Sixteen is an age to celebrate, I suppose."

"Of course it is," Elsie said. "Perhaps you will tell me what you are planning."

And so the three spent the morning in lively talk of birthdays and old friends and all the good times they had shared growing up.

After dinner that day, the girls joined Mrs. Carrington and her parents in the sewing room. Mrs. Carrington was cutting out work shirts for the field hands, and Elsie and Lucy took up scissors and pins to help. Herbert came after a while, bringing Elsie's *David Copperfield* with him, and while the women worked, he began the reading. Lucy and Elsie took a long walk in the gardens toward sundown, and after supper, Harry and one of his friends who was also visiting Ashlands, organized a horseback ride in the light of the full moon.

After such a busy day, Elsie was quite happy to excuse herself at her usual bedtime, and though she indulged, a little guiltily, in an extra half hour of chatting with Lucy, Elsie did not neglect her devotions and prayers before bed. She included a special plea that night for her friend Herbert, that he might be relieved of his terrible suffering.

The days at Ashlands were so full of activities that they seemed to fly past. On the Friday morning before the birthday party, Lucy proposed that she and Elsie should visit the kitchen and help with the cake baking.

Elsie, who like Lucy knew nothing of cooking save the eating, said, "Are you sure we won't be in the way?"

"Never," Lucy replied with assurance. "Aunt Viney will love to have our help."

As it turned out, Lucy was only half correct. Aunt Viney, who was widely known to be one of the best cooks in the entire county, certainly enjoyed the company of the two girls. But with a party to prepare for and a house full of guests to feed as well, she was not sure that this was the best day to be teaching the ways of the kitchen to anyone. Still, she and her staff welcomed the girls, and Aunt Viney tried to find them employment. Luckily, Chloe had come along too, and when she saw how much serious work there was to be done, she relieved Aunt Viney from the task of directing the girls.

"What do you want to make, young misses?" Chloe asked.

"Oh, everything!" Lucy exclaimed like a child on her first visit to a candy store. "Cakes for the party. White cake and yellow cake and sponge and fruit cake and—"

"I tell you what," Chloe said. "Let's us start on a sponge cake, like you suggest, Miss Lucy. That'll give you a good idea of what it takes to make a cake."

The girls plunged in with enthusiasm, learning about how to sift and measure flour, separate eggs into their whites and yolks and beat the whites into stiff peaks, cream butter and sugar, and prepare the heavy baking pans. They paid close attention and followed Chloe's instructions to the letter, and when their sponge batter at last went into the oven, both girls collapsed into rickety kitchen chairs.

"I never knew baking a cake was such hard work," Lucy said.

"Or that beating butter and sugar could make my arms hurt so," Elsie added.

"Or that a kitchen could be such a hot place," Lucy said as she wiped her dripping forehead with a handkerchief.

Hearing these remarks, Aunt Viney roared out her big, hearty laugh. "I guess you two learned a couple of good

lessons today," she said merrily while winking in Chloe's direction. "And one was how a sponge cake gets made. I 'spect you want to make another cake now. A nut cake maybe? I got a big bag of pecans over there you can start shelling and ...."

Lucy was already on her feet. "Oh, no, Aunt Viney. I mean, thank you very much, but Mamma needs our help, and we must be going." Lucy was pulling Elsie's arm by now. "We'll be glad to help some other time, I'm sure, but we really have to go now."

As the two girls disappeared out the kitchen door, nearly tripping over one another in their haste, they heard Aunt Viney's roar of a laugh once more.

"I just never knew," Elsie said breathlessly as they entered the house, "what labor it takes to make a meal."

"Nor did I," Lucy agreed. "But I will surely appreciate every morsel I eat from now on!"

And for the rest of the day, the kitchen at Ashlands hummed on, busy to be sure, but thankfully free of eager, young visitors.

The next day — the birthday — dawned bright and clear, and everyone was up early. Herbert was feeling much better, so after breakfast, Harry arranged a ride with Lucy and Elsie accompanying Herbert in the carriage. They didn't go far, for several of the party guests would be arriving for dinner at noontime, but Harry directed them to a pleasant, shaded grove where everyone alighted and Herbert could rest on the soft grass for awhile.

They returned just before dinner to find Carrie Howard and Enna Dinsmore already present. The contrast between these two was inescapable. Carrie, now seventeen, was a lovely and graceful young woman, mature in her manner yet totally unassuming. The sweet, open nature of her character made her a great favorite of young and old.

Enna, on the other hand, had changed little in nature from the conceited and demanding little girl who had caused Elsie so much trouble at Roselands. Enna had grown tall and was so self-possessed and worldly in her dress and speech that she seemed much older than her fourteen years, and she was always proud when strangers mistook her for a grown woman. When Horace was not around, she still assumed an attitude of superiority over Elsie, teasing and taunting the latter in a most unattractive way that was obvious to everyone except herself.

Elsie, however, usually tolerated Enna's rudeness. She sensed, somehow, that Enna was not a happy girl and that her outward boldness hid a sad heart.

In Lucy's room after dinner, the girls were admiring Lucy's birthday presents from her parents and talking about the party.

"How do you like my hair?" demanded Enna who had taken her seat, as might be expected, before Lucy's dressing table mirror. "It's the latest thing, you know. All the fashionable women in New York dress their hair this way now."

"It's very flattering," Lucy said, deciding she would have her maid copy the style for the party that night.

"And what do you think, Carrie?" Enna asked, patting at her own head of complicated braids and poufs.

"It's nice," Carrie said thoughtfully, "but excuse me for saying that it seems rather too grown-up for a girl of thirteen."

"Fourteen," Enna corrected. "Besides, everyone says that with my height and manners, I can easily be mistaken for eighteen."

"Perhaps," Carrie said softly.

"I see that you have done nothing to change your style," Enna went on, turning from her mirrored reflection to address Elsie. "I suppose your Papa commands you to keep your hair down and childish like that."

"He does not command," Elsie said, controlling her natural irritation at Enna's pompous tone. "He *wishes*, and so does Mamma, and I respect their judgment."

"I remember his reaction when you tried putting your hair up that day," Enna said with a little smirk.

"Oh, did you try, Elsie?" Lucy asked.

"Once, when Enna was visiting The Oaks, she convinced me to put my hair up with a comb. I quite liked it, but when Papa saw me — well, it was clear enough that he didn't find the style so pleasing. Mamma told me later that it was not the style to which he objected. He felt that it was not appropriate for a girl my age. And because he knows a great deal more about real fashion than any of us, I'll wait until he says it's time for me to wear a new style."

Lucy was giggling. "Do you remember that time when I asked for one of your curls, Elsie, and your Papa said I couldn't have it because it belonged to him?"

Elsie laughed too. "I thought he was going to be angry with me," she said, "but he wasn't at all."

"You are so meek," Enna said sarcastically. "No man would ever boss me that way. Why, if my Papa objected to my hair style, I'd tell him that it's my hair and not his concern."

"You wouldn't," Lucy said in astonishment.

"You could never be so impertinent to Grandpapa," Elsie added.

"Impertinent! And is it not impertinent for you to criticize your own aunt?" Enna demanded.

"You may be the aunt, but Elsie is older than you," Carrie said soothingly, "so she deserves the respect that goes with age."

Bested by Carrie's remark, Enna turned back to the mirror with a contemptuous sniff.

There was another little confrontation that afternoon. The girls had gathered with Herbert and Harry and Harry's friend in the parlor, and they were all discussing the plans for the party. Noticing that she was receiving less attention than Elsie, Enna blurted out, "I suppose, Elsie, that you will have to go to bed at eight thirty, or else your Papa will punish you."

The other young people looked at Enna, shocked at so ill-mannered a remark. Elsie, however, replied in a light tone, "No, Enna, I shall stay at the party till ten o'clock and enjoy every minute of it."

"But Elsie, our party won't be over till midnight," Lucy lamented. "Can't you stay up late, just this one time?"

"Of course, she can't," Enna sneered. "She is too afraid of her Papa to break his silly rules."

"Mr. Dinsmore's rules are quite intelligent," Carrie said, "and made to protect Elsie's health."

"And tomorrow is the Sabbath," Elsie explained, more to Lucy than Enna. "If I stay up late, I might oversleep, and I would surely be dull in church."

"The perfect little saint," Enna laughed. But seeing that she could not get a reaction from her niece, the haughty girl changed the subject, and not long after the group broke up to go to their rooms and dress.

Under Mr. and Mrs. Carrington's beaming smiles, the rest of the young guests arrived and were ushered into the beautifully decorated ballroom which had been created by opening the doors between two parlors. Every mantle and table was graced with vases of blossoms and greenery, and an abundance of candles flickered throughout, giving the room the feeling of a starlit summer garden. A harpist and pianist had been engaged to play the latest songs, and the young people mixed and mingled until someone suggested games. This proved to be much fun, especially for Herbert who was an ardent player at contests such as "Consequences" and charades.

Later, after supper had been served and enjoyed by all, Cadmus, the Carringtons' senior house servant, stepped into the room, fiddle in hand. At once, the word spread: "Dancing!" Country dances were a favorite pastime for the young people, so chairs and tables were quickly arranged against the walls as Cadmus tuned his old fiddle to perfect pitch. Then the dancing began with a rollicking reel.

Several young men begged Elsie to be their partner, but she politely declined. Instead, she found her way to where Herbert was sitting on a couch, watching the activity in which he could not take part.

She sat down beside him and said, "You will be my partner tonight, Herbert."

"But you mustn't miss out," he objected.

"May I tell you a secret?" Elsie asked, leaning closer so that she could not be overheard. Herbert nodded with interest, and she went on, "The truth is that I am not very fond of dancing. I love music, but I have never enjoyed dancing, even when I was a little girl. And I am not very good at it."

"But you are the most graceful girl I know," Herbert said with feeling.

"You have not seen me dance," Elsie laughed. "Please, let me stay with you here, and we can watch the others from a distance."

"Of course," Herbert said, not wanting to argue. In truth, he was overjoyed that Elsie had chosen to sit with him. As the music rose and the sounds of shuffling and tapping feet echoed through the room, Elsie watched her friends with rapt attention. Herbert's gaze, however, was drawn to another sight. After a while, he commented that the room had grown quite warm and asked Elsie to join him for a walk on the veranda. Happy that Herbert felt well enough tonight to walk unaided, Elsie quickly agreed.

Outside, a gentle breeze stirred the warm night air, and the still full moon was sufficient to light their path. The sounds of Cadmus's fiddling drifted outside and added to the happy mood. Elsie and Herbert talked easily, for they had always been kindred spirits, sharing interests and insights.

"How beautiful you are!" Herbert suddenly exclaimed, and so unexpected were his words that Elsie laughed.

"It's the moonlight," she said. "It makes everything beautiful."

"No, you are always beautiful," Herbert went on in a tone of the deepest sincerity. "In any light, you are the most beautiful girl I know. But tonight you look like a bride all bathed in white. I wish you were, and I were the groom."

The idea made Elsie laugh again. "Like two children playing dress up," she said gaily. "You are full of nonsense tonight, Herbert."

They were just passing the library door at the moment, and Elsie happened to hear the old clock there chime ten.

"Oh, dear, I must say good-night now. Enjoy the rest of your evening, Herbert. It's been a lovely party."

Herbert tried to stop her, but before he could catch her arm, Elsie was gone.

On the stairway, she met Mrs. Carrington.

"Not leaving so soon, are you dear?" the lady inquired, a look of concern coming over her face. "We are just about to serve the cakes and punch. You can't miss that."

"Thank you, Mrs. Carrington, but I really must get to sleep. Tomorrow is the Sabbath, you know, and I want to be rested for church."

"I understand," Mrs. Carrington said with a warm smile. "In your parent's absence, I will kiss you good night." Hugging the girl and kissing her forehead quickly, Mrs. Carrington said as she hurried down the stairs, "Sweet dreams, dear girl, and I will see you in the morning. I will be awake far too late myself tonight, so you may have to pinch me in church tomorrow to keep me awake."

~

Elsie had just entered her room and was turning up the wick of the oil lamp beside her bed when she heard a noise coming from the balcony. She jumped and turned frightened eyes toward the glass doors that opened onto the little terrace. A shadowy figure emerged from the billowing curtains. Arthur!

"What are you doing here?" Elsie demanded. "You weren't invited to the party, and it's not fit that you come into my room at this hour."

"It is not fit that you criticize your uncle and your elder," Arthur replied as he stepped into the room. "But to answer your question, I am here to collect the money you are going to lend me."

"I am not lending you any money."

"Give it to me then, and I won't have to worry about owing you."

"Give or lend makes no difference, Arthur. Papa has forbidden me to supply you with money of any kind."

Arthur's quick eye moved to the small purse that lay on the dressing table. "I already know you have enough in there," he said slyly.

Outraged, she cried, "You looked in my purse? Are you going to rob me?"

A twisted smile glided across Arthur's lips. "You always have money on hand for the needy," he said in a voice full of false sweetness. "Well, no one is more needy than I. You can give it to me with a clear conscience."

"You'll have to rob me first," Elsie replied defiantly. "And if you try, I will call the whole house to my assistance."

"And disgrace the family name by feeding scandal to the gossips?"

"If you care so much about the family name, Arthur, you will leave this instant."

Tiring of trying persuasion, Arthur moved toward the table and Elsie's purse. But just when he was about to take it, the sound of voices came from the hall, and he stopped. As the voices continued to come nearer, he ran back to the balcony door, empty-handed. He paused only to say one last thing to his niece:

"You think you're so good, you and Travilla, too. But *nobody* can refuse me and insult me as you've done and get away with it. I may not have your money, little Elsie, but I owe you something. And I will have my revenge. Trust me. The day will come when you will regret what you have done to me."

With that, he vanished. Elsie stood staring at the open balcony doors for almost a minute; then she rushed to them, slamming them closed and dropping the latches. Assured that she was now tightly locked in against another intrusion, she looked out into the night and suddenly began to tremble. She was standing like this a few minutes later when Chloe entered, followed by one of the Carringtons' maids who carried a silver tray.

"Mrs. Carrington sent these goodies up to you, Miss Dinsmore," the maid said cheerfully, "with her compliments."

Chloe, who had instantly noticed her charge's pale face and shaking hands, said, "Just put it there, Minerva, and I'll see she eats something. You go on back to the party."

The maid departed, and Chloe went to Elsie, gathering her beloved child into a strong embrace.

"What's happened, darling? You tell me exactly."

And Elsie did, pouring out the story and begging Chloe not to leave her.

"I'll be right here at your side," Chloe said, keeping her voice calm though her anger at Arthur was hot. "Don't you forget that the Good Lord is watching over you all the time, sweetheart, and I'm watching you too."

The nursemaid continued to hold Elsie for some time, until the terrible trembling passed and the girl's face regained its normal color.

Then Chloe took the cup of fruit punch from the tray. "You drink this down, darlin'," she said, and when Elsie raised her hand to push the cup away, Chloe was firm. "You drink it like I say. You had a dreadful shock, and that little glass of juice is gonna help you. Your Papa would say the same if he was sittin' here with us now."

CHAPTER

14

A Sudden Proposal

"Many waters cannot quench love; rivers cannot wash it away."

SONG OF SONGS 8:7

A Sudden Proposal

The next morning, all of the young people at Ashlands were allowed to sleep late, and Mrs. Carrington ordered that the breakfast bell not be rung so as not to disturb her guests. Even Elsie, who normally rose soon after the sun and needed no bell, slept until well past eight o'clock. Her devotion was perhaps a bit shorter than usual, and with Chloe's help, she rushed through her dressing. She arrived at breakfast just as Mr. and Mrs. Carrington and Mrs. Carrington's parents were being seated and a minute or two before Herbert.

"My dear," Mr. Carrington greeted Elsie in his jovial manner. "I am glad to see at least one of our guests this morning. It appears that you and Herbert will be our only young companions for church today."

Mrs. Carrington laughed and added, "Yes, we shall be a small party, I'm afraid. You were wise to retire early, Elsie. The party didn't end till after midnight, and it was at least another hour until I heard quiet from the guest rooms."

"It was a lovely party, and I know that everyone had a wonderful time," Elsie replied graciously. Then she turned to Herbert. "But you look very well rested for an honored guest."

Blushing slightly, the boy said, "I took advantage of being an invalid and went to bed not long after you left."

"How does it feel to be sixteen?" Elsie asked.

"Much as it felt to be fifteen," Herbert responded lightly. "But you will know soon. Your birthday is not many weeks away."

Elsie's New Life

"Let's hope it doesn't fall on a Saturday," Mr. Carrington said. "I don't think I approve of these Saturday night parties," he continued, looking down the table to his wife. "The young people really should not be allowed to miss Sunday services."

"Well, dear," Mrs. Carrington began in a soothing voice, "we can blame it on the calendar that Herbert and Lucy's sixteenth fell on a Saturday. And with Elsie to join us, we will have a good group for church this morning. The other children are to be up and dressed by the time we return."

In truth, Elsie was a little glad that the others were not coming to church. She had been frightened by Arthur's visit the night before, and she was still shaken by his threats. She doubted that she could keep up a cheerful appearance around Lucy and the others. Enna especially would be sure to sense anything wrong, and Elsie dared not explain herself to Arthur's sister, of all people. No, the story of Arthur's dreadful behavior would be for her father's ears only. Elsie would tell her Papa everything as soon as she returned to The Oaks.

The ride to the Carringtons' church was very pleasant, and their minister delivered an excellent sermon on courage. His words succeeded in calming Elsie and lifting her spirits. He spoke about the strength God gave Moses, Daniel, Esther, Elijah, and Jesus to be strong and stand before their enemies.

The other girls were indeed awake and dressed when the church-goers arrived back at Ashlands. Lucy, Enna, and Carrie were standing on the balcony as the carriages pulled up, and Carrie called down to Elsie and Herbert, "You make me feel quite ashamed. You've been to church while we have been lying in bed."

"Yes," Lucy added with a giggle, "we have been awfully lazy, and I suppose we must ask forgiveness. But wait there, and we will all go for a walk before dinner."

Before Elsie could reply, the three girls disappeared from their perch and soon reappeared at the front door. Enna, who could never resist a snide remark at Elsie's expense, said, "You are too good for words, Elsie. I'm sure you were up with the birds."

"Hardly," Elsie replied sweetly. "I overslept myself and was almost late to breakfast."

"Well, you must do penance for that, I suppose," Enna said with a haughty toss of her head. "But let's walk now. Are you coming with us, Herbert?"

"No," the boy answered. "I think I should rest this afternoon."

Lucy cast a worried look at her brother and saw that he did look a little pale. "Would you like us to stay with you?" she asked.

"No, no. You enjoy your walk. I'll just take a little nap before dinner."

Lucy, who well understood Herbert's sincere wish never to impose his fragile condition on others, slipped her arm around Elsie's waist and said cheerfully, "Then let's be off, ladies. I'm sure Herbert has no interest in our chatter, and we will see him later."

As the girls headed down the drive toward the gardens, Herbert slowly mounted the front steps, but at the door he turned to gaze at the laughing little group in their charming summer dresses. His attention, however, was directed to only one — the friend of his childhood who had become the love of his life. He watched her closely — her slim, tall figure, the graceful way she walked, her long brown curls that seemed to catch the glow of the sunlight. "She is the most wonderful person," he said to himself. "I must tell her today. I have to."

～～

After dinner, the girls gathered in Lucy's room, but when Enna suggested — insisted, really — that they spend the afternoon reading from a book of romantic poems she had brought, Elsie excused herself, saying that she was somewhat tired after all the excitement of the party.

"So we are not the only lazy girls in the house after all," Enna said with a sniff.

"Oh, do be quiet, Enna," Lucy snapped with more than a hint of irritation. "Elsie is *my* guest, and she may do as she pleases."

Carrie turned warm eyes on Elsie. "We have had more than our share of resting today," she said gently, "and you deserve yours. Shall we come and find you after we've read Enna's poems?"

"Yes, please. In an hour or so."

Elsie left Lucy's room intending to seek out her own room and to spend some time with her Bible. But suddenly she remembered Herbert. He had gone to the porch after dinner, and Elsie thought that he might want some company now. She was somewhat lonely herself, for she missed her parents especially on the Sabbath. The Carringtons were good Christians, but they did not share the habits of Elsie's own household. At The Oaks, Elsie knew, her father and Rose would be reading Scripture at this very moment, and later Rose would tell little Trip some of her wonderful Bible stories. There would be prayers, and in the evening her family and the servants would gather together for their devotion and hymn-singing. At The Oaks, the Sabbath was a full day of rest and worship and contemplation; at Ashlands, the Sabbath was divided between morning worship and pleasurable recreation for the rest of the day.

Elsie had learned from her father and Rose that dedicated Christians could differ about the manner in which they interpret God's commandments, and Elsie always tried to look into people's hearts rather than judging them by their practices. Still, she was uncomfortable when her friends read worldly books, played games, or took horseback excursions, as Harry Carrington was organizing for that evening, on the Sabbath. So she sought out Herbert who shared her dedication to spiritual pursuits.

He was on the porch, reclining on his couch and reading his Bible when Elsie approached.

"I'm so glad you came," Herbert said, a happy smile lighting his thin face. "But you don't have to keep me company, Elsie. I'm sure Lucy has more pleasant occupations planned. Don't let me stop you from having a good time with the others."

"Don't be silly, Herbert," she responded, taking her seat in a low rocking chair beside the couch. "I see what you are reading, and I will have the best possible time if we can read Holy Scripture together. That is what He wants us to do on the Sabbath, isn't it?"

"I believe it is," he said quietly. Looking at the book in his hands, he went on, "I find great comfort here, in His Holy Word. There are times, Elsie, when the pain is great and I have such rebellious feelings — especially when this disease makes me so helpless and weary of the pain. But He always helps me to bear it."

"You've reminded me of a quotation from Isaiah," Elsie said. "'In all their distress He too was distressed, and the angel of His presence saved them.' God feels our suffering with us, Herbert, so we are never alone in our pain."

The two young people sat silently for some moments; then Herbert asked, "Are you ever afraid, Elsie, that your troubles are too little and unimportant for God's notice? Do you ever worry about bothering or angering Him by constantly going to Him?"

Elsie looked into her friend's sad, questioning eyes and replied, "I asked my Papa that same question once, and I've never forgotten what he said. He asked if I ever thought any of my interests or problems were too trifling to tell to him. And I said, 'No, Papa. You've told me to come to you with any of my thoughts or feelings, and you are always interested in whatever I have to tell you, whether it be happy or sad.' I remember that Papa smiled and said, 'I am, dear, because you are so very near and dear to me.' Then he reminded me what the Bible tells us in Psalm 103: 'As a father has compassion on his children, so the Lord has compassion on those who fear Him.'"

"Yes, that's true," Herbert mused.

"And Papa also told me to think of God's infinite wisdom and power and how He keeps everything in motion, from the sun and all the solar systems to the tiniest insect. It's hard for us to comprehend even half of what He does! God doesn't make distinctions between the great and the small as we do. He attends to one and all at the same time, to all His creatures and all their affairs."

"It's a wonder to contemplate," Herbert said with enthusiasm, "to know that He knows everything, that He hears and answers all our prayers. Oh, I wouldn't trade that for anything, not even perfect health and all the wealth in the world."

"Yes," Elsie agreed, "because in Him, we have everything."

The two turned to Herbert's Bible and began reading aloud, taking turns with the verses. They would stop every now and then to discuss a passage or look up a reference. They were still deep in their study when a high-pitched and not altogether happy voice rang out.

"I am so bored with staying indoors and reading poems," Enna whined. She had just stepped onto the porch, with Lucy, Carrie, and Harry following in her wake.

"Then shall we take a walk before supper?" Harry asked.

"That's an excellent idea," Carrie said. "Will you come with us, Elsie?"

Before Elsie could open her mouth, Enna said mockingly, "Oh, she's much too pious to enjoy a pleasant walk with us on a Sunday. She objects to anything pleasant on her precious Sabbath."

"Indeed!" exclaimed Harry, casting a comical look at Elsie. "If that is so, Miss Dinsmore, then you must be consistent and object to yourself."

Elsie smiled. "Enna is mistaken. I find many pleasant things to do on the Sabbath."

Enna snorted, "Ha! Like going to church, and saying prayers, and reading that musty old Bible."

"Yes, Enna," Elsie said calmly. "All those things give me pleasure." She turned toward Lucy and went on, "You all enjoy your walk. Herbert and I will stay here and continue our lessons."

Brushing past Enna, Lucy went to her friend's side and bent forward to plant a soft kiss on Elsie's cheek. "We'll miss you," the girl said lightly, "but our loss is Herbert's gain."

Elsie's New Life

After supper, the young people hurried to the driveway where saddled horses awaited. The sun was still up, and the air was warm as all, save Herbert and Elsie, mounted for the ride Harry had arranged. After promising Mrs. Carrington that he would take only safe paths and have everyone back early, Harry led his little troop of riders off.

Herbert, who had not been able to ride on horseback since he was a small child, gazed a little longingly at his older brother. Harry sat so straight in his saddle, so tall and strong. It would not be fair to say that Herbert was jealous of his brother; in fact, he admired Harry greatly, for the older boy had always been his loyal guardian and protector. But Herbert wished that he might have a share of Harry's strength. Never before had Herbert been so conscious of his physical disability, of the frail body and weak legs that made him dependent on others. Tonight, of all nights, he wanted — needed — to be strong.

When the riders had gone, Herbert went back to the porch where Mrs. Carrington and Elsie had already taken their seats. The woman and the girl talked happily for some time, Herbert adding only an occasional comment, until Mrs. Carrington excused herself and returned to the house.

The sun was sinking, and the sky blazed briefly with brilliant roses and oranges and purples. Elsie and Herbert watched the display without speaking. As the color faded into twilight, Herbert said, "This has been such a happy day for me, Elsie. I have had you almost to myself. What a joy it would be if we could always be together like this."

A Sudden Proposal

"If only you were my brother," Elsie replied. "I've always thought of you as a brother, since we met as children."

"No! Not like that," Herbert exclaimed, startling Elsie with his vehemence. He went on in a rapid, urgent voice, "I have no wish to be your brother. I would be much dearer to you than that. Do you remember what I said last night? I wasn't joking, Elsie. I was never more in earnest. Oh, Elsie, could you ever like me enough?"

"But I do like you, Herbert, and I always have," Elsie said.

Herbert shook his head. "Not 'like'. I mean love. Could you ever love me — love me enough to marry me?"

Elsie's face suddenly flushed hot, and she stammered, "What are you saying? Marry? Why, we are both far too young to be thinking of such a thing. You're just sixteen, Herbert, and I'm not even that."

Herbert was adamant. "You are older now than your own mother was when she married your father. And what does age matter? Plenty of girls are married at sixteen, or at least engaged."

At that, Herbert turned his face away, and in the pale light, Elsie could see his shoulders slump. She wanted to comfort him but had no idea what to say.

His voice cracking with emotion, Herbert resumed, "Oh, dearest Elsie, I presume too much. You could marry anyone. You could marry a king if you cared to. Why would you want a helpless invalid like me?"

Elsie had never been so touched. "Stop talking so, Herbert," she said gently. "You are a good and noble young man, worthy of any woman in the land."

She reached out to lay her hand over his, and he grabbed it tightly, raising it to his lips.

"But can I ever be worthy of *you*?" he demanded. "Say I may, and I will be the happiest fellow in the world!"

At that moment, someone was lighting candles in the house, and the light fell across Herbert's face. In his eyes, Elsie saw something she'd never seen before — a deep well of passionate entreaty that moved her heart. And in her affection for this friend of her childhood, this kind and suffering boy who had endured so much with such grace, she forgot everything except her desire to comfort him and make him happy.

"Please tell me that there is some hope," Herbert pleaded. "Just tell me that you care for me and that someday you will love me and be my wife."

"I do care for you, Herbert, and I would do anything in my power to make you happy."

Herbert's eyes opened wide, and he again pressed her hand to his lips. "Oh, darling Elsie," he said in a hoarse whisper, "then I may call you my own. God bless you for your goodness!"

Elsie had no words. Her thoughts were twirling in confusion, and for a moment she felt faint. What had she done? What did Herbert expect of her? Nothing had prepared her for this moment. She wouldn't hurt Herbert for the world, but somehow she felt she had done him a wrong. What could she say now?

A vision seemed to appear in her head — her father's face. Her own dear Papa's loving face.

Gently, she pulled her hand from Herbert's grasp. Struggling to keep her voice steady, she said, "You must know, Herbert, that I cannot promise myself without my Papa's permission. I am still a child, his child, and I can do nothing of which he does not approve. Do you understand?"

A Sudden Proposal

"Yes, darling," Herbert replied, though in truth, his happiness was so intense that he barely heard her words.

Standing, Elsie said, "Then I must go now. I am . . . I am a little fatigued, and I think I should retire early. I'll see you in the morning."

As she retreated toward the door, his words came to her from the darkness. "Bless you, Elsie. You have made me the happiest person alive."

She could not bear to reply. Pretending not to hear, she rushed away to her room.

Fortunately, Carrie and Enna were leaving just after breakfast the next morning, and Harry was to accompany them on the journey. In the bustle of packing and loading and saying farewells, Elsie had no opportunity to speak to Herbert, and she was oddly relieved.

Enna and Lucy had dominated conversation over the breakfast table, and though polite and smiling as usual, Elsie contributed little. She was aware, however, of a sense of discomfort in the presence of all the Carringtons. She felt shy and vaguely hesitant, like a foreigner in a strange land. She hoped that it was only because she had not slept well the night before. But she wondered if Herbert had spoken to his parents or Lucy.

She got her answer as soon as the other guests departed. Lucy grabbed her arm and pulled her into the empty parlor. Shutting the door, Lucy wrapped Elsie in a tight embrace.

Laughing and crying at the same time, Lucy said, "You darling Elsie. You've made Herbert so happy. And me. We shall be sisters at last, Elsie dearest, really sisters! I don't think I've ever been so thrilled."

Elsie returned the embrace, then pulled back to look into her friend's radiant face. "But don't go putting the cart before the horse, Lucy. I can do nothing without Papa's consent."

"I know," Lucy said, growing serious, "and I understand. I've always thought your Papa to be too strict with you, but I understand that he must protect you in this, as my father would protect me. If he refuses his permission, I'll understand. Herbert is a wonderful fellow, just the kindest, smartest, most honest, and caring boy in the world. But his illness — his lameness — oh, it will not be easy for a wife."

Tears had come into Lucy's eyes again, and Elsie put her arm around her friend's shoulder, hugging her close. "Papa admires Herbert very much," she said. "He has often spoken of Herbert's courage in facing such pain. Whatever Papa decides, I believe it will be for Herbert's good as well as mine."

"I do hope your father will give his approval," Lucy said earnestly, "for Herbert's sake. But if he doesn't, I promise that it will not change my feeling for you, Elsie. You will always be my best friend."

"And you mine," Elsie said with great feeling.

The girls hugged once more, but Lucy suddenly hopped backwards, her eyes round as if she had been caught by surprise.

"I nearly forgot," she exclaimed. "Herbert is waiting for you on the terrace, and I promised to bring you straight out. He will be so annoyed with me."

They hurried to the porch and found Herbert sitting up in a chair and looking healthier than Elsie had seen him for some time.

A Sudden Proposal

"Good news seems to become you, Brother," Lucy laughed.

"Joy is a powerful medicine," he replied, rising with the help of his cane.

"I will leave you two for a while, unless you desperately want me to stay and entertain you," Lucy said teasingly. Since no answer was necessary, she hurried away with skipping steps.

When they were both seated, Herbert took Elsie's hand and looked into her eyes. "Have you changed your mind?" he asked.

"No, Herbert, but the decision belongs to Papa. You must ask him now."

"I have already done just that," he said.

"But how?" Elsie asked in astonishment.

"As you may imagine, sleep did not come easily to me last night. I was so happy," he squeezed her hand warmly, "that at first I felt as if I were in a dream. Then I realized that I must approach your Papa. It's not a task that I look forward to. I hardly think he will be pleased at the prospect of a cripple like me for a son-in-law."

"Don't say that, Herbert. Papa admires you greatly. He says so often."

"But he knows there is no promise that I will ever be better. I may never recover my health. And what then, darling, for you? I can't bear the thought of bringing suffering on you."

"But, Herbert," Elsie said in a soft whisper, "would you love me any less if I were to become ill or lame?"

"No! Never!" he exclaimed and slumped into his chair.

"Then tell me how you asked my father for his consent."

Sitting straight again, Herbert said in a steady voice, "I wrote to him last night. In fact, I wrote several letters until

I found just the right words. Never has a letter been so important to me. It was well past two when I finished, and as soon as the house began to stir this morning, I entrusted the letter to my servant to take to The Oaks. Your father should have it now."

"Then we have only to wait," Elsie said. "I'm sure it won't be long. Papa is not one to keep us in suspense."

It soon became clear that all the Carringtons had been informed of Herbert's proposal. No one made any direct comments, but at dinner, Mr. Carrington was smiling even more broadly than usual, and Mr. and Mrs. Norris several times brought up the subject of their own long and happy marriage. After the mid-day meal, Mrs. Carrington took Elsie aside for several minutes to express her hope that Horace Dinsmore would approve the engagement. She averred that, regardless of her motherly pride, there was no finer, worthier young man than Herbert, and Elsie readily agreed.

Of all the family, only Harry seemed to disapprove. He said nothing, of course, but several times Elsie caught him looking at her with a cold eye, and instead of his normal good nature, he appeared moody and taciturn. When he spoke to his younger brother, his tone was short, almost cross. Harry's attitude troubled Elsie, for she could not believe he would begrudge any happiness that might come to Herbert. She could not understand why he should be upset when the news seemed to bring such pleasure to everyone else.

A Sudden Proposal

Mrs. Carrington took her sewing to the porch that afternoon in order to chat with Herbert, Elsie, and Lucy. They talked of everything except the one subject that was at the front of all their minds. As the afternoon wore on and it became harder to avoid the topic of the proposal, Elsie prevailed on Herbert to read to them from *David Copperfield*. Listening to the story seemed to settle everyone's nerves, and Herbert had just started a new chapter when a servant appeared, announcing the arrival of a rider from The Oaks.

It was Jim, and he carried a letter for Elsie.

She took the envelope and opened it with trembling hands.

"It's from Papa," she said, quickly reading the contents. She looked up into Herbert's expectant face. "He says that I must return home immediately."

"Is there no word for me?" Herbert asked anxiously.

"He says that you will hear from him tomorrow morning. It is a very brief note, Herbert."

"But must you go?" Lucy gasped. "Your Papa promised that you could stay with us for a full week and that is not yet ended."

"I know," Elsie replied. "But his note is very clear. I must go now."

"Is your father angry?" Herbert asked. "I fear that this sudden change does not auger well for me."

"Oh, Herbert," Elsie said, moving to his side, "I'm so sorry to go, but I must obey Papa. Please don't leap to conclusions until you have heard from him tomorrow."

"Yes," Herbert said with a deep sigh, "you must obey your father. And I must be patient." Then firming his tone, he spoke to the young man from The Oaks. "Jim, you can go saddle Miss Elsie's horse now."

"Yes, sir," Jim replied. "And the cart will be here soon to gather Chloe and all the luggage."

"Oh, dear," exclaimed Mrs. Carrington. "This is most unfortunate. But you must do as your father commands, Elsie. Go to your room now and change into your riding things. We certainly don't want to annoy Horace, so we must let you go, I suppose. Tell Aunt Chloe that I'll send a servant up to help with the packing."

Not more than twenty minutes later, Jim was in the front drive, holding his own horse and Elsie's Glossy. Elsie had said all her good-byes except to Herbert who stood with her at the front door.

Taking her hand in his, he asked, "You will come again soon, won't you? And we'll correspond, won't we? I would like to write you every day until I can see you again."

"It all depends on Papa," Elsie replied in her kindest tone. "If he permits, then we will write each day, and I'll visit as soon as possible."

"And if he doesn't permit?" Herbert demanded.

"You must be patient, Herbert. And you must believe, as I do, that Papa will decide only what is best for both of us."

Herbert gazed into her eyes with such a forlorn look that at that moment, Elsie would have said anything to lift his spirits. But she restrained her impulse, knowing that raising false hopes would be more cruel than kind. She gave his hand a last squeeze, and with a whispered "Good-bye," she walked to her horse, mounted, and began the ride back to her home and her Papa.

CHAPTER

15

To Everything, A Season

"For there is a proper time and procedure for every matter, though a man's misery weighs heavily upon him."

To Everything, a Season

When Herbert's letter had arrived at The Oaks that morning, it had created much debate and discussion. Horace opened the letter at the breakfast table, and as he read, his wife immediately saw the change in his countenance.

"What is it, dear?" Rose asked worriedly as Horace at length laid the pages down. "I've rarely seen you looking so disturbed. Is it about Elsie?"

"It's ridiculous. Absurd," Horace responded, struggling to control his emotions. "Young Herbert Carrington is asking me for Elsie's hand in marriage! There! I have astonished you. What can these two children be thinking? I would have credited them with greater sense."

Rose was smiling now. "It certainly is a surprise, dearest," she said. "I had not thought of Elsie as old enough to contemplate marriage. But she is almost sixteen, and I've observed that many girls in this region are engaged by that age."

"Not Elsie!" Horace exclaimed as he unconsciously crumpled Herbert's letter in his fist. "I'll have none of this nonsense for years to come. Why, she shall not marry until she is at least twenty-one. No, twenty-five."

Laughing lightly, Rose said, "But, dear, don't you remember how old I was when we married?"

Horace flushed. "Twenty-one," he grumbled. He was on his feet now, pacing the floor.

"And what would you have done if my father demanded we wait another four years?"

Horace stopped by her side and leaned down to kiss her warmly. Recovering his smile, he said, "I would have fought like a tiger to make you mine."

"And what age were you when you married the first time? What age was Elsie's mother?"

"Don't tell me you support Herbert's ridiculous proposal?" Horace asked with considerable consternation.

"No, dear," Rose assured him. "I am only trying to point out that age is not a strong argument if you are to be consistent."

"You may be right. But age is not the only difficulty. Indeed were Herbert Carrington a strong and mature young man in vigorous health and if they agreed to a long engagement of four or five years —" He paused, considering the possibilities, then dropped into the chair beside his wife. "But I do not believe lengthy engagements are good," he continued. "And young Carrington's health? The sad truth is that he is unlikely ever to recover from his crippling illness and almost certain to die before he reaches twenty. The idea of Elsie becoming a widow while she is still just a girl . . . "

He raised his hand to his eyes as if to blot out the vision. "Can I allow my beloved child to sacrifice herself in such a way?"

Rose reached for his hand, pulling it away from his face and looking into his troubled eyes from the depth of her love. "It would indeed be a terrible sacrifice," she said softly, "but doesn't it depend very much on her feelings for Herbert?"

"But is she old enough to know her feelings?" Horace asked. "Does she not need more time for her taste and judgment to mature before she chooses a companion for life?"

"I believe you're right, my dear," Rose agreed. "I only want you to consider Elsie's feelings in this, and Herbert's as well. I know that you will be kind and gentle to them both."

He kissed her again. "Thank you, my dearest," he said softly, "for allowing me to give vent to my distress. You're right, as always. I cannot reply to young Carrington in anger, and I must speak to Elsie before I communicate with him. The final decision is mine, but I must know her feelings before I take any action. I shall have her come home immediately."

"That's wise, dear husband. I know that you will be able to judge her true feelings when you look into her eyes."

For one of the few times in her life, Elsie did not look forward to a reunion with her father. She wondered if he would be angry or disappointed with her. Would he understand the confusion she felt?

Horace was waiting on the veranda when Elsie rode up. He rushed forward, helping her off her horse, and took her in a loving embrace that immediately dispelled her fears. He led her to a seat on the veranda and took his place on a bench opposite her.

"Now, tell me what this is all about?" he began gently. "Do you love Herbert?"

"Yes, Papa," she replied, "I have always loved him as a brother since we were little children. And I pity him so. He suffers dreadfully, and I would do anything to make him happy."

Horace looked into her eyes as she spoke, reading meaning there that Elsie herself did not comprehend. "I see," he said. "But, Daughter, do you think that the feelings you have for Herbert are those of a wife for a husband? Love for a husband is very different from love for a brother and a friend. Do you love Herbert more than you love me?"

"Oh, no, Papa!" she responded instantly. "Not half so much! But he is such a good person, and I cannot bear to hurt him."

"That is because you are a good person. But you must ask yourself if you would really be doing the best for Herbert if you do not have the right kind of love for him."

Elsie looked at him questioningly.

Horace went on: "Someday, my child, you will find a man whom you will love even more than you love me. And because your love will be so great, you will be ready to leave me and your Mamma and your home and to make your life with that person."

Elsie protested, "But that could never be possible, Papa, for I love you better than all the world."

Horace smiled. "And I am glad of it, dear," he said. "But when you meet the right person, you'll know it without any doubt or fears. You will love *him* best in all the world, and I will be happy for you. Of course, I hope that day doesn't come for a number of years yet," he added with a little laugh. Then he sobered and continued:

"Elsie, I can see into your heart, and what I see there is your affection and concern for a dear friend who suffers terribly. I know that you want to give Herbert some degree of happiness, but this is not the way to do it. In the end, a marriage between you will only bring suffering to both sides. Do you understand what I mean?"

"I think I do, Papa. I've been so confused since Herbert made his proposal. I was afraid to say no to him, but I was also afraid that I was wrong to accept him. And I didn't know why."

"Not wrong, dear. Just unwise. And I can promise you that when you find the person you are meant to marry, you will feel no confusion or doubts."

To Everything, a Season

As Elsie's father was speaking, she had felt as if a weight were being lifted from her. It was as though she had been saved from falling off the edge of a cliff. But one thing troubled her still.

"Papa, how will you tell Herbert that there is no engagement?" she asked.

Horace considered for a moment. "I will write to him, and you will read my letter before I send it. Believe me, Elsie, I have no wish to grieve that poor, brave boy any more than is necessary. And if he requests, I will meet with him, man to man as he deserves. But I want to write him immediately so that he will not gather false hopes from any delay."

Just at that moment, Elsie remembered her last conversation with Herbert. She grabbed her father's arm and said anxiously, "I told Herbert that I would write to him if you gave your permission. Shall I write, Papa?"

"No," Horace replied decisively. "No writing and no more visits to Ashlands for some time. It is the best way if Herbert is to get over this thing quickly."

Seeing her worried expression, Horace added, "I will explain in my letter that there is to be no communication. If Herbert needs to blame anyone, it will be me."

"Thank you, Papa," Elsie said, lowering her eyes to her lap. "It is sad, though, that I must lose a friend like this. I will miss seeing Herbert."

Horace rose and taking Elsie's hand, lifted her up. She slipped her arm through his and laid her head against his shoulder.

"What are you thinking now, dear?" he asked as they walked into the house.

"That I'm very glad to be home again," she said.

Elsie's New Life

Horace's letter arrived at Ashlands the following morning as promised. It was indeed a kind and considerate reply, as Elsie herself attested after reading it, but it brought no comfort to Herbert. He was distraught, and if he had had the ability, he would have ridden directly to The Oaks to plead his case in person. Instead, he wrote back to Horace, urgently requesting a meeting. Horace obliged, and rode to Ashlands the very next day.

Herbert petitioned for Elsie's hand in words more eloquent than Horace had ever heard from so young a man. It became clear that Herbert did love Elsie deeply and had loved her for many years. Realizing that on Herbert's part, the proposal of marriage was not a childish act, Horace was sincerely moved and did his best to ease the boy's grief. But he was firm in refusing to allow the engagement and in cutting off communication with Elsie. Unwilling to leave no hope, however, Horace assured Herbert that letters and visits might be exchanged at some time in the future.

"Understand, my boy, that this is not a rejection of you," Horace said. "I admire you more than any young man I know. But Elsie is far too young and unprepared for the responsibilities of marriage, and I would reject any suitor for her hand. I appreciate the strength of your feelings for her, and that is why I think it best to cut off communication for the time being. The day may come, I hope, when you can resume your relationship as friends, and I will revise my position accordingly."

"Then you do not blame me for loving her?" Herbert asked.

To Everything, a Season

"Never, sir, for you have treated my daughter with honor and respect," Horace replied with the utmost sincerity. "But I must go now. Believe me, Herbert, I am sorry to be the cause of your disappointment, and I wish only the best for you."

"Good-bye, Mr. Dinsmore," Herbert answered with surprising strength in his voice. "And thank you for being so honest with me."

A month or more passed. Elsie celebrated her sixteenth birthday quietly with her family, and though she thought of Herbert often, it was with compassion rather than regret. She followed her father's wishes and made no attempt to contact anyone at Ashlands — an action made a little easier when she learned from Carrie Howard that all the Carringtons had traveled North to take Herbert to a specialist in New York. Elsie also began to understand what her father had told her, that true love such as Horace and Rose felt for each another cannot be made out of sympathy alone. Rose was a great comfort, helping Elsie to realize how life changed as one grew older and persuading her that although other girls might marry young, it was not the best course for everyone.

One day toward the end of summer, Enna came for an unexpected visit. Horace was away, for which Enna was grateful since her brother tended to silence her self-indulgent prattle. She found Rose and Elsie in the sewing room, where little Trip was playing with a set of toy horses at his mother's feet. Enna plopped herself on the couch without a word of greeting.

Elsie's New Life

"Have you heard the news?" she demanded.

"No," said Elsie. "What news?"

"First, there is Arthur. Father has caught him out. He has been gambling and got himself up to his ears in debt. I thought Papa might kill him when he discovered the truth, but Arthur was *soooo* sorry and pretends to be *soooo* penitent that Papa has paid his debts and forgiven him. Arthur and Walter both leave for college next week, and Papa seems to think that Walter can keep his errant son on the straight and narrow. I'm grateful not to be in Walter's shoes."

When Elsie and Rose had no reply to this news, Enna went on, "Arthur seems very angry with you, Elsie. He says you could have saved him from being caught, but you wouldn't. What was that all about?"

"He asked me for money, but I wouldn't lend it to him because Papa forbade me to."

"And you always do what your Papa says," Enna said with a sneer. "Oh, no. That's not true. I forgot the time you almost died rather than obey my brother."

Elsie flushed, and Rose was starting to speak, but Enna rattled on, "My second piece of news is about Herbert Carrington. He's very ill and not expected to live. The family is in New York, you know, and the doctors there give Herbert little chance of surviving the year. I wonder what has caused him to fade so fast?"

For once, there was no hidden insult in Enna's question, but Elsie dropped her sewing to the floor. "How do you know this?" she asked in a quivering voice.

"Lucy wrote about it to Carrie Howard," Enna replied. "I'm surprised she hasn't written to you."

Elsie leaned forward to gather up her sewing items; instead, she rose from her seat and dashed from the room.

"What ever is the matter with her?" Enna asked Rose. "Is she in love with Herbert or something?"

"No, she is not," Rose replied in a firm, even tone. "But she values his friendship very much, and your news was very abruptly delivered."

Little Trip had come to the couch and was reaching toward Enna when she noticed him. She drew back and carefully smoothed down her skirt. The little boy, catching her unspoken signal, quickly moved away and returned to his mother's side, receiving a warm hug in that quarter.

"Elsie is such a cry baby," Enna snorted. "Always has been and always will be, I imagine."

"If she is crying, it is in sympathy for a friend," Rose said. "I think it is a trait you might well emulate, Enna. She controls her temper extremely well, and she has certainly put up with more from you than I would."

"What are you saying?" Enna demanded, anger flushing her face a bright red.

"I mean that Elsie is older than you, yet you treat her as a child. Your manner to her is often contemptuous, and you taunt her for behavior that should rightly earn your praise. You sneer at her for honoring her principles and obeying her father."

Enna stood up and with a sharp toss of her head, proclaimed, "Nobody would dare boss me the way Horace does her!"

"And you are so much the worse for lack of obedience," Rose said quietly, turning back to her stitches.

Enna hardly knew what to do. She wanted to voice her indignation and flounce from the room, but since Rose was paying no attention and little Trip had returned to his toys, the dramatic effect would be lost. She hesitated for a moment to sulk and was on the point of making a sharp remark to Rose when the door opened and Horace entered.

He greeted his wife and sister, then took Trip into his arms and sat on a comfortable chair, putting his son on his knee.

"Where is Elsie?" he asked.

"Crying in her room, I suppose," Enna said disdainfully.

"And why should she be crying?"

"Because I told her that Herbert Carrington is very ill and about to die in the North."

"Is that true?" Horace asked his wife.

"Carrie Howard received word of it in a letter from Lucy," Rose replied, "so I believe it is so."

Looking concerned, Horace put Trip down from his knee and stood. "It was good to see you, Enna," he said to his sister. "Here, I'll show you out. You should be going home before it gets dark."

Flustered but never without words, Enna exclaimed, "It is just after three o'clock, Horace!"

"Ah, but the night is coming earlier and earlier," he said, taking hold of her elbow and guiding her out of the room. "Your mother will be looking for you."

Having seen Enna safely mounted on her horse and trotting down the drive, Horace hurried back inside and went straight to Elsie's room. She wasn't there after all, but Aunt Chloe was.

At his inquiry, the nursemaid said, "I saw her heading outside, Mr. Horace, not ten minutes ago. No, sir, she wasn't crying, but she wasn't happy either. I bet she's gone to her arbor."

Chloe was correct. A few minutes later, Horace came into the little clearing and found his daughter sitting on her

favorite arbor seat. He approached quietly and took his place beside her.

She looked at him, and he could see that she was dry-eyed, but her face was full of sorrow.

"I have heard about Herbert," he said.

"I feel as if I had killed him," Elsie said in a whisper. "If he dies, it will be my fault."

Torn by her sadness, Horace hugged her close. "There is hope yet, Elsie dear. There is always hope. And even if the worst occurs, it can never be your fault. Remember that it was I who caused that poor boy's disappointment. That is my responsibility. But there is something more important for you to remember. Herbert's life is in God's hands, not ours. We must pray for him and love him, but whatever happens, it will be according to God's plan."

At his words, Elsie's tears did fall. Horace said no more but held her close until her weeping had ceased. And then father and daughter joined in fervent prayer for the boy who had suffered so much in his short life.

Several months later, in the late afternoon of a late autumn day when the trees had lost their leaves and all the earth seemed to be preparing itself for another winter's sleep, a letter from New York arrived at The Oaks. A servant brought it to the dining room where the family was having supper. It was addressed to Elsie in a hand she did not immediately recognize. There were several pages, and Elsie looked to the final one to find the signature. The name of the writer surprised her.

Dear Elsie,

I am sorry to be the bringer of such sad news, but my brother Herbert passed away last night, and I believe with all my heart

that he is now at peace in the arms of our Heavenly Father. He was courageous to the end, but his pain is over at last, and he has entered an eternity of happiness.

I wanted to write to you immediately so that you would not receive this news from others. More than anything, I beg you to feel no guilt or responsibility. Your affection meant everything to Herbert, and though his proposal to you was rejected, your love gave him the strength to face this final illness with grace and dignity. I can tell you now that his doctors had not thought he would live past fifteen, so I can only believe that the last year and a half of his life was a gift to all of us from God. You lightened all those months for him, Elsie. You gave him something to live for, and almost to the end he believed that someday he might recover and be able to ask again for your hand.

When you were last at Ashlands, that day everyone learned about Herbert's proposal, I fear I acted badly, and you may have mistaken my motives. I was not angry with you, dear friend. But I knew Herbert's condition, and I was terribly afraid that you would accept his proposal without being told of all the circumstances. In fact, I was angry with my parents whose hopes for a miracle had blinded them to the truth. They believed you might save him. I was afraid that you would sacrifice yourself to his illness.

Your father is a very wise man, and I hope you have never blamed him for rejecting Herbert's proposal. Your father did what was right, as even Herbert came to understand after a time. Not long before he died, Herbert told me that he would have acted just as Mr. Dinsmore did if he were your father. "Elsie is the finest person I know" he said, "and the day will come when she finds the real love of her life, and if I could, I would be the first to dance at her wedding." He meant that. He *wanted you to be happy always, just as you had made him so happy.*

Please trust me, Elsie. You could not have prevented his dying. But you added so much to his living. I will always be grateful to you for each day of sunshine you gave him.

The funeral will be held in two days, and Herbert will be buried here, in a site that overlooks the Hudson Valley. His grave will face the sunset. Be happy for him. He is with God, and I know he is walking tall and straight.

> *Your faithful friend,*
> *Harry Carrington*

Elsie's eyes were brimming with tears when she finished the letter. Carefully, she folded the pages, and then handed them, with the envelope, to her father.

"It's from Harry Carrington," she said, and her voice carried no trace of tears or weakness. "I want you and Mamma to read it. It's about Herbert. He has died. But it's a wonderful letter all the same."

"Are you alright?" Horace asked, his own voice cracking slightly.

"I am, Papa," she said thoughtfully. "And do you know something? I know that Herbert is alright too. Read the letter, Papa, and you'll understand."

She rose from the dining table, and smiled at her father.

"If you don't mind, I'd like to go to the arbor for awhile. I think I'd like to watch the sunset tonight."

Will an old enemy become a new threat?
Is Elsie about to make a fateful decision?
What deceitful traps lie ahead for her?

Elsie's story continues in:

ELSIE'S STOLEN HEART

Book Four of the
*A Life of Faith:
Elsie Dinsmore* Series

Available at your local bookstore

Collect all of our Elsie Dinsmore books and companion products!

A Life of Faith: Elsie Dinsmore Series

Check out
www.alifeoffaith.com

- Get news about Elsie

- Join the Elsie Club

- Find out more about the 19th Century world Elsie lives in

- Learn to live a life of faith like Elsie

- Learn how Elsie overcomes the difficulties we all face in life

- Find out about Elsie products

A Life of Faith: Elsie Dinsmore
"It's Like Having a Best Friend From Another Time"

— ABOUT THE AUTHOR —

*M*artha Finley was born on April 26, 1828, in Chillicothe, Ohio. Her mother died when Martha was quite young, and James Finley, her father, soon remarried. Martha's stepmother, Mary Finley, was a kind and caring woman who always nurtured Martha's desire to learn and supported her ambition to become a writer.

James Finley, a doctor and devout Christian, moved his family to South Bend, Indiana, in the mid-1830s. It was a large family: Martha had three older sisters and a younger brother who were eventually joined by two half-sisters and a half-brother. The Finleys were of Scotch-Irish heritage, with deep roots in the Presbyterian Church. Martha's grandfather, Samuel Finley, served in the Revolutionary War and the War of 1812 and was a personal friend of President George Washington. A great-uncle, also named Samuel Finley, had served as president of Princeton Theological Seminary in New Jersey.

Martha was well educated for a girl of her times and spent a year at a boarding school in Philadelphia. After her father's death in 1851, she began her teaching career in Indiana. She later lived with an elder sister in New York City, where Martha continued teaching and began writing stories for Sunday school children. She then joined her widowed stepmother in Philadelphia, where her early stories were first published by the Presbyterian Publication Board. She lived and taught for two years at a private academy in Phoenixville, Pennsylvania — until the school was closed in

Elsie's New Life

1860, just before the outbreak of the War Between the States.

Determined to become a full-time writer, Martha returned to Philadelphia. Even though she sold several stories (some written under the pen name of "Martha Farquharson"), her first efforts at novel-writing were not successful. But during a period of recuperation from a fall, she crafted the basics of a book that would make her one of the country's best known and most beloved novelists.

Three years after Martha began writing *Elsie Dinsmore*, the story of the lonely little Southern girl was accepted by the New York firm of Dodd Mead. The publishers divided the original manuscript into two complete books; they also honored Martha's request that pansies (flowers, Martha explained, that symbolized "thoughts of you") be printed on the books' covers. Released in 1868, *Elsie Dinsmore* became the publisher's best-selling book that year, launching a series that sold millions of copies at home and abroad.

The Elsie stories eventually expanded to twenty-eight volumes and included the lives of Elsie's children and grandchildren. Miss Finley published her final Elsie novel in 1905. Four years later, she died less than three months before her eighty-second birthday. She is buried in Elkton, Maryland, where she lived for more than thirty years in the house she built with proceeds from her writing career. Her large estate, carefully managed by her youngest brother, Charles, was left to family members and charities.

Martha Finley was a remarkable woman who lived a quiet Christian life; yet through her many writings, she affected the lives of several generations of Americans for the better. She never married, never had children, yet she left behind a unique legacy of faith.